MIND YOUR OWN
BUSINESS, KRISTY!

**Other books by
Ann M. Martin**

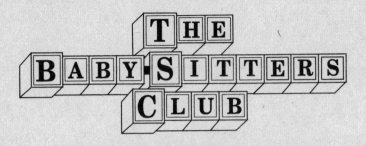

MIND YOUR OWN BUSINESS, KRISTY!

Ann M. Martin

AN
APPLE
PAPERBACK

SCHOLASTIC INC.
New York Toronto London Auckland Sydney

Cover art by Hodges Soileau

No part of this publication may be reproduced in whole or in part, or stored in a retrieval system, or transmitted in any form or by any means, electronic, mechanical, photocopying, recording, or otherwise, without written permission of the publisher. For information regarding permission, write to Scholastic Inc., 555 Broadway, New York, NY 10012.

ISBN 0-590-69213-5

12 11 10 9 8 7 6 5 4 3 2 1   7 8 9/9 0 1 2/0

Printed in the U.S.A.   40

First Scholastic printing, April 1997

*The author gratefully acknowledges
Peter Lerangis
for his help in
preparing this manuscript.*

MIND YOUR OWN BUSINESS, KRISTY!

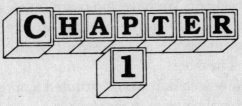

CHAPTER 1

"I'm free!" I shouted.

I closed the front door behind me and ran into the kitchen. It was Friday afternoon. School was over. Spring vacation had begun. I was ready to celebrate.

So was our puppy, Shannon. She jumped all over me, yipping happily.

Sitting around the kitchen table were Porky, Arnold, and Piglet. Actually, they were my three brothers — Charlie, Sam, and David Michael. At least I assumed they were. I couldn't see their faces. They were practically buried in a bowl of chips and pretzels.

Charlie's seventeen, Sam's fifteen, and David Michael's seven. During snack time, though, they enter a time warp. *Dzzzzt* — transformed into greedy two-year-olds. I could have been King Kong and they wouldn't have noticed me.

"Please, don't all say hello at once," I said,

1

throwing the day's mail on the table.

The radio was blaring in the background. "This is Donnie Donaldson on WSTO, bringing you a beeeeootiful spring day in Stoneybrook, Connecticut. We have mo-o-ore music and another ticket giveaway coming up later, so get ready to send us a postcard with yourrrrr phone number!"

"Waw weh dah woo?" grunted Sam, sending a spray of chips onto the floor.

"Ewwww!" shouted David Michael.

Crunch, went my footstep on some pieces of chip. "Saaa-aaam!" I cried out.

Sam swallowed. "I *said*, 'Why don't you enter that one?' You know, the ticket giveaway."

Charlie rolled his eyes. "Sweepstakes are for suckers. Your odds are, like, a million to one."

"Kristy entered the last one," Sam said.

"Figures," Charlie grumbled.

"You did?" David Michael asked.

"Yes," I said defiantly. "But only because it was for a Blade concert."

Sam grimaced. *"Blade?* Yuck."

I ignored the comment. I love my brother, but he has no taste in music. Blade is my new all-time favorite rock group. They are the coolest. Personally, I think you'd be a sucker *not* to enter a free-ticket sweepstakes for Blade.

"Uh, Sam, would you please clean up your mess?"

2

"Shannon will eat it," Sam said.

"Shannon hates chips," I reminded him.

Sam reached for a sponge. "Bossy, bossy, bossy."

I was not offended. Do you know how many times I, Kristy Thomas, have been called bossy? At least a zillion. It's okay. See, I think bossy is a code word. When a *boy* is forceful and responsible, people say he's "strong-willed" or "a born leader." But if you're a girl, you're "bossy."

Frankly, I take it as a compliment.

I think of myself as the strong, silent type. Well, maybe not so silent. I tend to speak my mind. A lot.

Okay, the strong, loud type.

Trust me, when you have a family the size of mine, you have to be loud. How big is my family? Sixteen. Three grown-ups, seven kids, and six pets.

It's a good thing our house is so big. You might even say it's a mansion. My stepfather, Watson Brewer, is a millionaire. But don't picture a snobby guy with a year-round suntan and mirrored sunglasses. He's quiet and balding, and he likes to garden and cook.

The third grown-up in our house is my grandmother, Nannie. She moved in with us after Watson and Mom adopted my adorable two-and-a-half-year-old sister, Emily Michelle, who was born in Vietnam. Watson's two kids from a previous marriage live with us during alternate months. (Karen's seven and Andrew's four.) This month they were with their other parents, the Engles.

Age-wise, I'm somewhere in the middle. Which kind of makes me the hub of the family (ahem). I'm thirteen, although if you saw me you might guess younger. I'm just over five feet tall. My friend Stacey thinks I should wear shoes with heels or lifts. My friend Claudia thinks I should fluff up my hair to create an illusion of height. Fat chance. The Kristy Thomas motto: Comfort over fashion. I think jeans and T-shirts look and feel great, and I like to wear my hair pulled back into a ponytail. Why change a perfect combination? End of argument.

Here are some other things you need to know about me: I love sports, especially baseball. I'm in eighth grade at Stoneybrook Middle School. I am the founder and president of the Baby-sitters Club, or BSC, which I will tell you about later.

In case you're wondering — yes, I have a biological dad. Yes, he's alive. And no, I don't know exactly where he is. His name is Patrick and he abandoned our family soon after David Michael was born. Mom says that my dad "had problems connecting." As far as I can figure out, that means two things: (1) he couldn't hold down a job, and (2) he couldn't stand the pressures of parenthood and marriage.

Needless to say, things were tough after he left. But good old Mom pulled through (with a lot of help from Charlie at first, and then Sam and me as we grew older).

On that Friday afternoon, Mom and Watson were in the backyard, puttering around in the garden. In the kitchen, Sam wiped up his spat-out chips, Charlie shuffled through the mail, and I opened the fridge. I dug out a butterscotch pudding and a bottle of Yoo-Hoo and brought them to the table.

Charlie was ripping open an envelope. He pulled out a glossy brochure and read aloud: " 'Wissahickon College . . . We mold today's thinkers into tomorrow's leaders.' "

David Michael made a face. "They put *mold* on you?"

"It means they make you into a leader," Sam explained.

"They all say that," Charlie said with a sigh.

"Boring," David Michael commented. "Go to a college that'll make you an astronaut."

Charlie flipped through the other envelopes. "Rhineback School of the Arts . . . Levithan Polytechnic Institute . . . I've never heard of these places. How am I supposed to pick one?"

"Go to Stoneybrook University," Sam piped

up, "so you can live at home and drive us around."

"Yeah!" David Michael agreed.

Charlie raised an eyebrow. "Hmmmm . . . where's that University of Alaska brochure?"

He was kidding (I think).

You would not believe how many colleges have sent him brochures this year. Maybe a hundred. I didn't blame him for being confused.

Slurping my Yoo-Hoo, I picked out the one envelope addressed to me. It was a catalog from Bouncy Bottoms Baby Boutique.

Why, you may ask, did I receive that? Because of my ex-sort-of-boyfriend, Bart Taylor. You see, we each coach a kids' softball team, and my team was once sponsored by a diaper service company. Well, we're not sponsored by the company anymore, but back then Bart thought it would be hilarious to put my name on Bouncy Bottoms' mailing list.

Har har.

Bart and I are still friends. We used to be something, well, more. Not ever exactly boyfriend and girlfriend. But *he* thought we were, so we had to cool things off. Sort of break up, so we could be just plain pals. Does this make sense? I guess you could say Bart and I have a real seesaw relationship.

So do the Krushers and I. They're my team.

Sometimes they're gung-ho, but lately they'd been very ho-hum. I was at wit's end trying to figure out why.

A bored team, an obnoxious ex-sort-of-boyfriend, a brother headed for Alaska. Good thing it was spring vacation. I needed something positive in my life.

I tossed the Bottoms brochure into the trash and started looking through my mom's J. Crew catalog.

Rrrrrring!

"I'll get it," I said.

It was almost four o'clock. Our Friday Baby-sitters Club meeting was going to start in an hour and a half. I figured a frantic member was calling to tell me she'd be late.

I picked up the receiver. "Brewer/Thomas residence."

"HELLLLLLLO!" The voice was so loud that I had to hold the phone away from my ear. "IS THIS KRISTY THOMAS?"

"Yes," I said. "Who's — "

"THIS IS DONNIE DONALDSON FROM WSTO, AND YOU ARE THE WINNER OF OUR HOT TICKET GIVEAWAY!"

I smelled an Alan Gray moment.

Alan is the Goon King of the Eighth Grade, and he loves to play stupid phone jokes. I could hear the radio in the background, and Donnie Donaldson was *not* speaking on it.

"Alan, you are the worst mimic I ever heard," I said. "I hear they give lessons in Antarctica. Why don't you move there?"

"YOU AND THREE OF YOUR LOVED ONES WILL BE OUR GUESTS AT THE STAMFORD CIVIC CENTER FOR A CONCERT FEATURING THE MUSIC OF . . . BLAAAAADE!"

I nearly choked.

That last word had echo, or reverb, or whatever you call it. Alan couldn't do that on his phone.

"You mean — I — I *won?*" I stammered.

My brothers scrambled out of their chairs. They stood close to me, their ears cocked toward the phone.

"JUST TELL US THE NAME OF YOUR FAVORITE RADIO STATION!" Donnie Donaldson honked.

"Double-you-ess-tee-ohhhh!" my brothers and I shouted at the same time.

"THAAAAAT'S RIGHT! LOOK FOR YOUR TICKETS IN THE MAIL!"

"Oh, wow! Oh, I don't believe this! Thank you!" I gushed.

"WE LOVE YA, KRISTY! SEE YOU AT THE ARENA!"

The phone went dead. I dropped it in the cradle and leaped into the air. "Yyyyyyyyesss!"

"Yeeeaaaaaa!" Sam and David Michael were doing victory dances across the kitchen.

Mom and Watson came bounding in from the backyard. When they heard what had happened, we all formed a big hugfest.

Well, all except Charlie. He wasn't saying anything.

I grinned at him. "Sucker, huh?"

"Sorry." Charlie's face was red. "I could drive you, you know. I really like Blade."

"Can I go?" David Michael asked.

"The concert's too late, honey," Mom said.

"Don't worry, I'll stay home with you," Sam volunteered. "Blade stinks."

"Blade *stink*," I corrected him.

"Then don't go," Sam replied.

"No, I mean — " I waved a hand at him. "Never mind."

"Make it a double date," Mom suggested. "You and Bart, Charlie and Sarah."

"Sarah yes, Bart no," I said.

"Uh, Sarah no, too," Charlie said softly.

I wasn't expecting to hear that.

"You guys broke up?" I asked.

Charlie nodded and grabbed some more chips.

"Oh . . ." I felt awful. I liked Sarah. We all did. She and Charlie had been together for the longest time.

9

I wanted to ask questions, but I could tell Charlie didn't want to talk. He looked about as comfortable as a mouse in a field of catnip.

He muttered, "It's really no big deal," and slunk toward the living room.

We all looked at each other. No one knew quite what to say.

Except David Michael.

He was beaming. "*Now* can I go?"

CHAPTER 2

*R*rrrrring!

I barely heard the phone. Claudia Kishi's radio was turned up full blast. The moment I'd told all my Baby-sitters Club friends that I'd won Blade tickets, *click!* On went the radio. Now they all wanted to enter the next ticket giveaway.

The clock read 5:29, a minute before starting time. Claudia was passing around a bag of Cheez Doodles and a box of caramels. Abby Stevenson and Mallory Pike were dancing. Jessi Ramsey was doing ballet stretches to the beat. Stacey McGill and Mary Anne Spier were sitting on Claudia's bed, completing a crossword puzzle.

Rrrrrring!

I flicked off Claudia's radio. As I picked up the phone, the clock clicked to 5:30.

"Order!" I shouted.

"Oh, dear," said a familiar voice over the phone. "Did I call Pizza Express?"

"Uh, no, not Pizza Express, Mrs. Kuhn, the Baby-sitters Club," I replied. "I was just, you know, calling the meeting to order."

Everyone was cracking up. I could not keep my face from turning red.

"Oh. Well, I know it's short notice," Mrs. Kuhn said, "but I need a sitter for tomorrow, about noon."

"I'll see what we can do and call you right back."

The moment I hung up, Abby exploded with laughter. "One baby-sitter, extra cheese with pepperoni?"

"Is that a deep-dish sitter, or a Sicilian?" Claudia asked.

I ask you, is this any way to treat the club president? Hmmph.

Ignoring the comments, I calmly repeated Mrs. Kuhn's request to Mary Anne. She ran her finger down the BSC record book. "Let's see . . . Mal and I are at the Pikes', Stacey has the Hobart kids, Kristy's sitting for the Papadakises . . . Abby, you've got a doctor appointment . . . Claudia's available, but Jessi hasn't had a job in a few days."

"I'll do it," Jessi agreed.

I picked up the phone and called back Mrs. Kuhn to confirm.

Pretty efficient, huh?

In the BSC, we don't mess around. That's why we're so successful.

I should know. I invented us.

Why? For the same reason Edison invented the lightbulb and McDonald's started making burgers. To fill a Big Need.

Back in the Dark Ages of Stoneybrook, busy parents had to waste time calling individual sitters. Including my mom one evening, back before she married Watson. Neither Charlie, Sam, nor I was available to baby-sit for David Michael. After about an hour's worth of phone calls, Mom was fed up, and my mind was cooking.

I thought: If Mom were calling a taxi, she wouldn't call the individual drivers at their homes. She'd call a central number.

Fanfare. Drumroll. History in the making. The Baby-sitters Club was born.

We started small — just Claudia, Mary Anne, Stacey, and me. But parents loved us, and they spread the word. We had to expand fast. Nowadays we have seven regular members, two associates, and one honorary member.

We meet every Monday, Wednesday, and Friday in Claudia's bedroom from five-thirty to six. Our clients know that's the only time they can reach us all. Why Claudia's? Because she's the only BSC member who has a private phone line.

Watson calls us a high-volume business. The "high-volume" part can be tricky. With so many clients, we can't guarantee each family the same sitter. So it's important to trade information about our charges. I require all BSC members to write about every single job in an official club notebook, which we read at meetings.

The "business" part is no sweat. We're a well-run company, with rules, officers, and weekly dues. Our dues help pay Claudia's phone bill and reimburse my brother Charlie for driving Abby and me to meetings. We also buy supplies for Kid-Kits, which are boxes of toys, games, and books we take with us to jobs.

As club president, I run the meetings, dream up new publicity ideas, and organize most of the events for our charges. Claudia calls me an Idea Machine.

It's one thing to think of an idea such as the BSC, but it's another thing to make it run. That's why our secretary, Mary Anne Spier, is so important. She controls the official record book, which contains our calendar and client list. When a call comes in, she needs to know exactly who's available to baby-sit. Which means she has to record all our conflicts in advance — doctor, dentist, and orthodontist appointments; lessons; family trips; and after-school activities. In the back of the book, she keeps our client list updated with addresses, phone numbers, rates paid, plus tons of special information about our charges' likes and dislikes.

Tough job, huh? Well, Mary Anne enjoys it. Ever since we were babies, she's loved to organize things. (She used to build elaborate cities out of blocks. I would drive a toy truck through them.)

Do you know the song "The Wind Beneath My Wings"? That's how I feel about Mary Anne. And not only in terms of the BSC. Mary Anne and I are absolute best friends. When my dad ran out on my family, she really stood by me. She is the kindest, most sympathetic person I know.

I have a theory about why Mary Anne is so sensitive. It's because her life began so sadly. You see, Mrs. Spier died soon after giving birth to Mary Anne. Richard, Mary Anne's dad, was so devastated that he sent Mary Anne to live with her grandparents. Big mistake. They didn't want to give her back. They were afraid Richard was too grief-stricken to be a good parent. But he put his foot down, brought his daughter home, and spent the next twelve years trying to be Superparent. He meant well, but he treated Mary Anne like a fragile little baby. As late as seventh grade she had to wear Pollyanna-type clothes and keep her hair in pigtails.

Don't worry, Richard grew up. Mary Anne is allowed to look her age. Nowadays she has a short hairstyle and wears neat, preppy-style clothes. (Otherwise, she looks kind of like me — five feetish, with brown hair and brown eyes.)

Mary Anne has a stepfamily now, too. The BSC helped that happen. Awhile ago we took in a member named Dawn Schafer, who had moved to Stoneybrook from California with her divorced mom and younger brother, Jeff. Dawn's mom had grown up in Stoneybrook, and guess who her high school sweetheart had been? Richard Spier! Mary Anne and Dawn reintroduced them, and — *tsssss!* — the flame was still burning. Mr. Spier and Mrs. Schafer were married, and the Spier family moved into the Schafers' huge old farmhouse.

Dawn and Mary Anne grew close, but Dawn became homesick for California and moved back to be with her dad. Jeff had done the same thing earlier, so now Mary Anne's a solo kid again. She misses her stepsister a lot (so do the rest of us), but Dawn is great about phoning and writing. She visits a lot, too — and when she does, Claudia makes sure to stock up on veggie chips and dried seaweed and other disgusting snacks. Dawn's a health food fanatic.

Claudia's the opposite. Vice-president is the perfect position for her because she has a huge vice: junk food. She hides candy, cookies, chips, pretzels, and cupcakes all over her room. Her parents would faint if they knew. They are the Nutrition Police of Stoneybrook. (Literature Police, too. Believe it or not, Claudia has to hide her Nancy Drew books because they're not "serious reading.")

How does a human sugar worshipper look? Zit-free and gorgeous. I don't understand it. Claudia could be a model. Let me be more specific. She looks like a thirteen-year-old Japanese-American model with long black hair, a constant smile, and weird clothes.

What do I mean by weird? Well, that Friday, for instance, she was wearing an old fringed leather vest she'd found in a thrift shop; an oversize plaid shirt with a super-thick striped tie; and bell-bottomed pants with two different-color legs. Her hair was pulled back with a hairclip in the shape of a VCR.

Everyone complimented her on how cool she looked. Me? I kept wanting to press the eject button to see if a teeny cassette would pop out of the hairclip. (I should never have admitted that to Claudia. She calls me style-deficient.)

Claudia is one of a kind. Her artistic talent is amazing. She can paint, draw, sculpt, and make jewelry like a pro. The talent doesn't carry over into schoolwork, though. I think the Art section of her brain is so huge that it swallowed up the Math, Spelling, and Science sections in one big gulp. She fell so far behind this year that she was sent back to seventh grade. Sigh. I miss having her in my classes, but at least she's finally receiving good grades. And it's great to see her confidence grow.

The other Kishis are real brains (especially her older sister, Janine the Genius), so Claudia needs all the self-confidence she can get. Her grandmother, Mimi, was the only one who really understood her. Ever since Mimi died, Claudia has kept a picture of her on her wall, for inspiration.

Claudia's other vice-presidential function (besides supplying junk food) is answering stray phone calls during non-meeting hours.

Our treasurer is Stacey McGill. She collects dues every Monday and adds up all our funds. Stacey loves numbers. She happens to be the top math student in the state. (It's true. She won the title in a Mathletes competition.)

She also happens to be Claudia's best friend. They like to talk fashion. Stacey doesn't wear VCRs in her hair, though. She always looks as if she just stepped out of a *Sassy* or *YM* cover. Personally, I think she wears too much black, but she insists it "sets off" her blonde hair. Whatever.

Stacey says that if I'd grown up in New York City like she did, I'd have a fashion sense, too. (Which is sort of like saying that wombats could speak if they went to school.)

Stacey's parents are divorced. They were still married back when the McGills first moved to Stoneybrook. They came here because Mr. McGill's job had transferred him to Connecticut. Stacey settled in, joined the BSC, and *whoosh* — the company transferred Mr. McGill back to New York. Well, Stacey's parents hadn't been getting along, and all the moving pushed them over the edge. Next thing we knew, Stacey was back in Stoneybrook for good, with her mom.

Post-divorce life has meant lots of shuttling between NYC and Stoneybrook (a pretty short train ride), but Stacey can take it. She's tough. Looking at her, you'd never know she has a serious health condition. It's called diabetes. Her body can't handle sugar. Too much (or too little), and she could become very sick, even pass out. Diabetes is controllable, though. Stacey has to eat meals at regular times, stay away from sweets, and give herself doses of a hormone called insulin. (She has to inject it, but she assures me it's not as gross as it sounds.)

Abby Stevenson is the BSC's other New Yorker. She was born and raised on Long Island. Now she lives two houses away from mine, with her mom and her twin sister, Anna. (Her dad died in a car accident when she was nine, but she hardly ever talks about him.) When I saw them moving in, I couldn't believe my good luck. Dawn had left for California, the BSC was overloaded with work — and suddenly *two* eighth-grade girls appeared on my street! We asked them both to join the club, but Anna said no. She didn't think she'd have enough time. She practices violin for hours every day. (Beautifully, too. I can hear her from my house.)

Oh, well, one out of two isn't bad. Abby turned out to be a great sitter. She's hilarious, for one thing. She's great at sports, for another (a little undisciplined, if you ask me, but lots of natural ability).

What you notice first about Abby is her thick nest of curly dark brown hair. Or maybe her bloodshot eyes and reddened nose. Abby is allergic to just about everything. She has asthma, too, and needs to carry around inhalers in case of an attack.

Abby couldn't be more different from her sister. Anna the Musician is quiet, thoughtful, and serious. Abby the Comedian is wild and loud. (Nonmusical, too. You should hear her sing. No, I take that back. You shouldn't, if you value your hearing.) The one time I saw Abby truly serious was at her Bat Mitzvah. That's a ceremony Jewish girls go through at age thirteen, and it involves lots of studying and a recitation in Hebrew.

Abby is our alternate officer. She takes over for any officer who might be absent. (Which doesn't happen too often.)

Not all of us BSC members are thirteen. Jessi Ramsey and Mallory Pike, our junior officers, are eleven years old and in sixth grade. They're best friends, too. We call them "junior" because their parents won't allow them to baby-sit, except for their own brothers and sisters, at night. This isn't a problem, though. They do a lot of afternoon sitting, which frees the rest of us for nighttime jobs.

Jessi is African-American. She moved to Stoneybrook, which is mostly white, from a racially mixed community in New Jersey. The adjustment wasn't easy. I didn't realize bigotry existed in Stoneybrook, but it does. Fortunately, things have smoothed out. The Ramseys are a strong family, but I sure wish they hadn't had to go through that. Jessi has an eight-year-old sister named Becca and a baby brother named John Philip (everyone calls him Squirt).

Jessi's hair is always pulled back tightly into a bun, to keep it out of her face when she dances. She's a fantastic ballerina, and she takes lessons in Stamford (Stoneybrook's nearest city).

Mallory and Jessi have much in common. They are both addicted to books about horses. They're both the oldest kid in their families. And they're both creative. Mal's talents are writing and illustrating. She wants to be a children's book author when she grows up.

Mal is Caucasian, with reddish-brown hair and freckly skin. She has to wear glasses and braces, both of which she hates. Her family is huge — eight kids altogether, including triplets.

Our two associate members are Shannon Kilbourne and Logan Bruno. They don't have to attend meetings or pay dues, but they fill in for us whenever we're overloaded. Logan is Mary Anne's boyfriend. Unlike Mary Anne, he's kind of a jock, involved in lots of after-school sports. Shannon's the only BSC member who goes to one of the local private schools, Stoneybrook Day, and she's in a million different activities herself.

Okay, enough about us. Back to the meeting.

While I was talking to Mrs. Kuhn, confirming Jessi's sitting job, a loud crash sounded in the background. As Mrs. Kuhn was hanging up, I could hear her yelling, "Jake, how many

22

times have I told you not to play with the soft-ball near the African violets!"

I couldn't help laughing. Jake and his two sisters, Laurel and Patsy, belong to the Krush-ers. Jake's always been a little . . . coordination-challenged. He had been improving, though, before the team sank into their latest group funk.

Oh, well, at least he was playing with the softball. That was a good sign.

After I hung up, I turned to Jessi. "Make sure you work with Jake on his fielding."

"The last time I was there," Jessi said, "all three of them wanted ballet lessons."

"Work it in," I suggested. "They can wear their mitts. You know, spin . . . catch. Pirou-ette . . . throw."

Jessi looked horrified.

"No, huh?" I said.

"Bring the Kuhns over to my house," Mal-lory suggested. "Mary Anne and I will be there, Kristy. Mary Anne's going to be sitting and I'm going to be around. We can play soft-ball in our yard."

That wasn't a bad idea. Not at all.

But I could feel the Idea Machine churning out a better one.

Ka-ching!

"I know!" I said. "A clinic! The first annual

23

Krusher Spring Klinic. We'll gather the whole team at Stoneybrook Elementary. We'll have batting and fielding drills, calisthenics, base-running contests. If they practice every day during spring break, we might be in shape for the season."

Mallory and Mary Anne were looking pale. "We wouldn't actually have to . . . do any softball ourselves, would we?" Mary Anne asked.

"I'll help coach," Abby volunteered.

I picked up the BSC record book, which was open to the calendar. "I figure one practice a day, around noon — "

"Well, I've got that doctor appointment tomorrow," Abby said. "And on Thursday, Mom's taking us to Pennsylvania. . . ."

"No problem," I replied. "I'll get Bart to help out. This'll be perfect. He can bring some of his team over, boost up that competitive edge. Maybe we can even schedule a few preseason games — "

"Uh, Kristy?" Stacey said. "This is supposed to be a *vacation*."

"Next stop, the Super Bowl," Claudia said, pulling a bag of Milk Duds from behind her bed. "Here, Kristy, have a milk product. It'll calm you down."

Abby was howling. "The Super Bowl is football, Claudia."

"Don't give her any ideas," Jessi piped up.

"Okay, so I can count on Abby," I said. "Who else?"

"I'll help," Jessi volunteered. "I guess."

Not enthusiastic. But better than nothing. I picked up the phone and began tapping out the numbers of my team members. If I expected them to be there the next day, I had to start right away.

Spring training right here in Stoneybrook.

I loved it.

CHAPTER 3

"What do you mean, you can't help coach the clinic?" I said into the kitchen telephone.

"Don't shout, Kristy," answered Bart Taylor.

"I'm not shouting!"

"It would be weird, Kristy, that's all. I mean, we're opponents. All the stuff I do with my players — batting tips, positioning, coaching signs — you'd be learning all my secrets."

"Secrets? Bart, it's only a game!"

Bart laughed. "Is this Kristy the Competitive talking? Look, I told the Bashers we'd have our own clinic this week. At the Stoneybrook Day field. They're looking forward to it, sort of a team preseason."

I took a deep breath. "No problem, Bart. I can find plenty of coaches. See you."

The truth? Without Abby and Jessi, I had no other prospects. Claudia still can't figure out which hand to put a mitt on. Stacey hates softball. Mary Anne and Mallory will watch a practice happily, but they'd rather eat a cactus than actually participate.

"Hi," said my brother Charlie, bouncing into the kitchen. He yanked open the fridge and pulled out a box of raisins, a bag of green grapes, a bottle of Coke, and a tub of Cool Whip. "You look grumpy. Another fight with your boyfriend, Alan Gray?"

"Ha-ha. It's just Krusher stuff."

Charlie plopped down on a chair and dipped a bunch of grapes in the Cool Whip. "Want some frosted grapes?"

"Nahh." I was still pretty full from dinner. Besides, I was too anxious to eat.

Charlie was scarfing down frosted grapes and soda. From upstairs, I could hear Nannie singing Emily a lullaby. The kitchen clock read 9:05, which meant Watson and Mom were still at the movies. Sam and David Michael were outside, playing some kind of explorer game with a flashlight.

"I have a new plan," Charlie announced. "Clown college. It really exists. They teach you how to do mime and juggling and stuff."

"You can't do any of that!"

"Wrong. Guess what I'm imitating?" Charlie began puckering and unpuckering his lips, eyes wide open.

"A fish?"

"Bart Taylor kissing my sister!"

I threw a grape at him. "Low, Charlie. Very low. For your information, good old Bart refused to help me coach the Krusher Klinic, and it's starting tomorrow."

Charlie swallowed a handful of frosted grapes. "*Now* he tells you?"

"Well, I only thought up the clinic idea today. But I've already called all the Krushers."

"Do the coaching yourself," Charlie suggested. "You don't need him."

"Sure, Charlie. I'll pitch to the kids. Then, when they miss, I'll run behind them and retrieve the ball. If they hit it, I'll instantly appear in the outfield to coach the fielders. And in the meantime, I'll play catch in foul territory with the others. No problem."

"So call it off. No one will kill you."

"Are you crazy? These kids need the practice. They're rusty. They have no energy. We can't start the season like that — "

"I could help you," Charlie said.

"Especially if Bart is going to have a Basher clinic — " *Screech* went the brakes in my head. "Wait. What do you mean? You know someone who'd do it?"

"Yeah," Charlie said with a shrug. "Me. All I'm doing this vacation is hanging out and pretending to look at colleges."

"You mean it? You would come to the clinic

every day and run drills and teach the kids and cheer them on?"

"Sure. I like kids. Why not?"

I let out a loud whoop. "You are the greatest brother!" Honestly, I almost kissed him.

"And," Charlie said with a proud smile, "I may be able to arrange a visit by the Mets' famous all-star third baseman, Jack Brewster."

"Yeah, right."

"Seriously. I know someone who is super-close to him. Can you see it? The kids'll go nuts. They'll never forget this the rest of their lives."

"Do you think you can really do it?" I asked. "I mean, he *is* a celebrity. He's probably got product endorsements and fantasy camps and stuff all lined up for the summer."

Charlie shrugged. "Well, I'll try."

"I won't mention it to the kids until you find out. Anyway, who is this person who knows Jack — ?"

Charlie sprang up and grabbed the bottle of Coke, which was now empty. "Ladieeees and gentlemen, Buddy Barrett steps up to the plate. Due to the expert coaching of Charlie Thomas and Jack Brewster, Barrett has brought his batting average up seventy points. Heeeere's the pitch!" He tossed up a grape and smacked it with the bottle.

The grape went sailing toward the sink. It bounced off the edge and rolled toward the door.

In ran Sam. *Splat* went the grape.

"Eew, what was that?" he asked.

"A mouse," Charlie replied.

Sam's face went white. He quickly lifted his foot to see.

"Made you look, made you look," Charlie taunted.

Sam grabbed a spoon from the utensil drawer and scooped out some Cool Whip. Holding it like a catapult, he took aim at Charlie. "Die, alien invader!"

Charlie took off like a shot, with Sam on his tail.

I sat down and picked at the grapes. I couldn't help smiling.

Okay, I knew the Jack Brewster thing was unrealistic. Definitely worth a try, but not likely to happen. Still, the clinic was a go. And I would be running it with my big brother. My big, goony brother, who was about to disappear to some college and probably never write.

I would never admit this to him, but in a funny way I was already starting to miss Charlie. Watching him read all those college brochures was giving me knots in the stomach.

It would be fun to do something major together. Charlie is a great athlete. He taught me all the basics of baseball when I was little. He knows how to give advice without making you feel stupid. Maybe I should have asked him earlier to coach the Krushers, but the idea never crossed my mind. Never in a million years would I have thought he'd want to help me with the clinic.

I dipped myself a big bunch of frosted grapes.

I was very, very lucky.

And so were the Krushers.

CHAPTER 4

"Great catch, Karen!" Charlie called out. "Except for one thing."

Near third base, my stepsister nodded. "I know. It was a hi, not a gimme."

"Yup!" Charlie cupped his hand to his mouth, and five Krushers stared at him intently. "Okay, everybody, let's practice. The ball is over your shoulder!"

Up went every glove, as if they were all waving hello. "*Hiiiiiii!*" they shouted together.

"Now the ball is coming to you waist high!" Charlie shouted.

The kids held out their gloves as if serving a dinner plate. "*Gimme!*"

I applauded. "Way to go, Krushers!"

I told you Charlie would be a great coach. It was 11:55, five minutes before the official start of the first Krusher Klinic, and he was already running a fielding practice. He was holding his official National League bat, wearing his baseball cap brim-sideways, and wearing a white batting glove. He looked like a pro.

My stepsister, Karen, was playing third base. My stepbrother, Andrew, was behind second. Nine-year-old Linny Papadakis was at first base, and his sister Hannie (who's seven) was playing shortstop. David Michael was in right-center.

Yes, the Krushers are a multi-gender, multi-age, multi-everything group. The only requirement is that you must want to play softball.

As I unloaded our equipment, Charlie hit a grounder to second base. " 'Hi and gimme,' huh?" I said. "I don't remember learning that."

"You never needed to," Charlie replied. "I did. Dad taught it to me."

Did I tell you my dad once played for a minor-league team? Well, he did. (I don't know many details. Maybe he left the team without notice. Ahem.)

Charlie's grounder went right through Andrew's legs. He turned around and watched it, as if it were some kind of interesting bird. "Nice try, Andrew, but you have to chase after it!" Charlie said. "Okay, we'll try again. Then everyone gets a ground ball, one by one! Be ready!"

The kids instantly leaned forward, legs bent, hands on knees.

I was impressed. First of all, I usually have to

beg them to take fielding positions. Second, I still don't have enough bat control to hit ground balls precisely aimed at a player. Charlie was doing it with ease.

As he batted, I set up the infield bases and gave tips to the players. What a great combo.

Before long, the rest of the team had arrived — Jake, Patsy, and Laurel Kuhn with Jessi; the Pike tribe with Mallory and Mary Anne; Matt Braddock, Jackie Rodowsky, Jamie Newton, and Nina Marshall with their dads; and Buddy and Suzi Barrett with their mom.

You should have seen their faces when they saw Charlie. They were in awe. It was as if Babe Ruth himself had appeared on the field.

I couldn't blame them. Charlie's seventeen. He's kind of handsome (for a brother), very athletic, and strong willed . . . er, bossy. (If this was their reaction to Charlie, I knew they'd go nuts over Jack Brewster. Boy, did I hope he could come.)

I caught a glimpse of Scott and Timmy Hsu running onto the field with a tall, high-school-age girl. She had long, light-brown hair and was dressed in tight jeans and a waist-length suede jacket.

"Who's that?" Jessi whispered.

"I've seen her in my neighborhood a few times. She's in high school. Her name's Monica or Jessica or something," I replied.

I was starting to feel impatient. Now that the whole team had arrived, it was time to start our official Krushers warm-up. "All right, Krushers!" I yelled. "Let's do some stretching — "

"Jake — first base!" Charlie barked. "Hannie — second! Buddy — center!"

One by one the players ran into place.

How many listened to me? None.

"Uh . . . hello?" I said.

Jessi was cracking up.

Oh, well. We could stretch after the practice. It felt kind of nice for someone else to be taking charge.

"Okay, long ball!" Charlie shouted. "Go deep! Deep!"

The kids in the outfield scurried back. Charlie tossed the ball straight up, then grabbed the bat with both hands. Gritting his teeth, he took a huge swing — and missed.

"Heyyyy, batter, that was a nice fat pitch!" I teased.

Charlie's face was turning red. He gave me a tiny smile. And then his eyes flickered over toward Harmonica or Harmony or whatever her name was.

She giggled.

Gag me.

Charlie tried again. This time he hit a towering fly ball to deep center field. Linny raced underneath it.

Along with Buddy, Suzi, Karen, and Timmy.

"Someone call for it!" Charlie shouted.

"I got it!" That was Jackie. He was running backward from the infield, toward the other kids.

Not one of them saw him. Not one of them backed away. They were all looking straight up.

I cringed.

Thud.

"OWWWWWW!"

The ball bounced onto the grass. So did all of the players, in a big heap.

A run-and-hit accident, courtesy of Jackie Rodowsky. (Jackie's nickname, by the way, is The Walking Disaster. The "Walking" part is optional.)

Timmy was crying. Karen was clutching her side. I ran toward them, along with a bunch of sitters and adults.

"Are you all right?" I asked Karen.

"I landed on Jackie's knee," Karen replied. "Ow ow ow."

"Sorry," Jackie said sheepishly.

I knelt to help Karen up. I figured Charlie might offer to help, too. But he was leaning over Timmy, comforting him. Shoulder to shoulder with Seneca or Veronica or whoever.

"Uh, Charlie? Your sister hurt herself," I said loudly.

Charlie spun around. "Oh! Anything serious?"

"Probably just a bruise," Karen said.

"Jackie, you don't call for the ball unless it's near your position," Charlie gently scolded him.

By now the team had gathered around to gawk. "All right, everybody back to positions," I said. "Karen and Timmy will sit out for awhile."

The kids all stood there, watching their two teammates limp off the field. "Go ahead!" I commanded.

"Okay, this half of the team line up for batting practice!" Charlie bellowed, with a chopping motion through the middle of the crowd. "The other half spread out on the field!"

Zoom. Instant obedience.

"You guys don't listen to me like that," I grumbled, trudging into foul territory with Karen.

We sat on the bench and watched the batters take turns. When each one stepped up, Charlie would shout one-word instructions, such as "Feet!" or "Legs!" or "Elbow!"

And you know what? The batters knew exactly what to do — straighten out their feet, bend their legs, lift their rear elbows.

Charlie had good technique, I had to admit.

Good, but flawed. A kids' softball team is not an army troop. Kids need individual attention.

When four-year-old Jamie Newton went to bat, Jessi helped Charlie set up the batting tee. Then Charlie barked Jamie into a decent batting position.

The only problem was, he was on the wrong side of the plate.

I ran over to them. "Charlie, he's a lefty!"

Gently I tried to move Jamie to the other side. But Jamie refused to budge. "No! Charlie told me to do it this way!"

"Jamie, we've been doing it the other way since you started," I insisted.

"But he's the boss!" Jamie pleaded.

"Says who?" I blurted out.

"Uh, Kristy's right, Jamie," Charlie said gently.

"Okay." Jamie hopped over to the other side of the plate.

I smiled. I patted Jamie on the head. I trotted into the outfield to coach the kids.

I was grinding my teeth the whole way.

As I stood out there, deep in center field, all the kids were poised around me. In fielding positions. Just the way I'd always told them to be. The batters were lined up quietly. On the sidelines, the sitters and parents were chatting away. Jessi was sitting with Karen and Timmy. Cressida or Spartacus, whatever her name was,

was sitting at the edge of the wooden bench, looking intently at my brother.

The Krusher Klinic was starting off with a bang. The kids were full of energy. I should have felt thrilled. Grateful. But I didn't.

I felt totally useless.

CHAPTER 5

Sunday

Day two of the Krusher Klinic.

Kristy, you are a genius. I have never seen the Pike kids so excited about softball. Herding them out of the house has never been easier. They enjoyed practice so much. Right, Mal?

Two, four, six, eight, who do we appreciate? Kristy! Kristy! Yeeeaaaa!

Mal and Jessi were going a little overboard. They were trying to make me feel good. I guess Jessi could tell I was disturbed after Saturday's practice.

Don't I have great friends?

Actually, by Sunday I'd gotten over my gloom. As I ate my pre-Klinic lunch, I could hear David Michael, Linny, and Hannie playing catch in the backyard. Softball fever was in the air.

I'd called Klinic for noon again. It was already 11:35, and Charlie wasn't home. He was supposed to drive David Michael and me to the playground, but he'd disappeared with the car earlier. I figured it had broken down (it's a real junker).

Across town, Jessi was strolling along Slate Street. She could hear the song "Take Me Out to the Ballgame" blaring from the Pike house.

She followed the sound to the backyard. The Pikes were in the middle of a softball practice, while a boom box played from the picnic table.

If you ask me, an eight-kid family is just about perfect. You can actually field a full softball team, if a parent pitches. Which was exactly the situation Jessi found at the Pikes'.

Well, sort of. Mr. Pike was pitching, but only seven Pike kids were in the field. Mallory the

Sports Hater was sitting on the picnic bench, making sketches.

Okay, sports fans, heeere's the Pike lineup: Leading off in age, after Mallory, are the triplets, Byron, Jordan, and Adam, who clock in at ten years old. Next is nine-year-old Vanessa, followed by Nicky, at eight. A perky seven-year-old, Margo is the penultimate Pike, with youngest honors going to Claire, who's five. (I love that word, penultimate. Sportswriters use it all the time. It means next-to-last.)

"Hi, Jesserina!" Mr. Pike called out. (Get it? *Jessi* plus *ballerina*? Grown-ups can be so corny.)

"Hi!" Jessi replied. She waved to everyone as she sat next to Mal. "Who are you drawing?"

Mal held up her sketch: a kid with a sideways-turned baseball cap. "Can you guess?"

Jessi looked around the yard. All the kids were wearing sideways-turned baseball caps. "What's with the hats?"

"That's the way Charlie wears his," Mallory answered. "They all want to look like him. Anyway, the drawing's supposed to be Adam."

"Clai-*aire*, hurry up!" Nicky was calling from the outfield. "It's almost time to leave for the Klinic!"

Claire was stamping down the dirt around home plate (a plastic container lid). Jessi noticed that she had a frilly white glove on her right hand.

"Why are you wearing that?" Jessi asked.

"It's a batting glove," Claire answered.

Mal nodded. "Charlie wears one."

Claire planted her feet, swung the bat around a few times, and spat.

Just like you-know-who.

Well, almost. Usually Charlie's spit flies out in one piece. Claire's was more like drool.

"Eeeewwww!" Margo cried out.

Claire tried to wipe off her mouth, but she slimed her glove.

Mr. Pike was struggling not to crack up. The other kids didn't even try. They were howling. Screaming. Rolling on the ground.

"You silly-billy-goo-goos!" Claire screamed.

Mr. Pike scooped her off the ground before she could burst into tears. "We'll wash up. The rest of you get ready to go to Klinic!"

Mal and Jessi gathered the kids together and waited out front. When Claire emerged, she was wearing a green–and–yellow–polka-dot mitten.

"Take Claire out to the ba-a-allgame," Adam sang, "watch her spit on her glo-o-ove . . ."

"Stop!" Claire cried.

"Buy Adam peanuts and Cracker Jack," Vanessa continued. "He'll grow so fat that he'll fall on his back."

"Hey!" Adam bellowed.

By the time they arrived at the playground, the Pikes were chasing each other around.

I was already there, playing catch with Buddy and Suzi Barrett.

"Hi, guys!" I shouted. "We're going to start with throwing and catching. Everyone gather behind home plate."

I might as well have been speaking Greek. The triplets were trying to corner Vanessa. Claire was trying to bite Adam. Nicky was teaching Margo how to do cartwheels.

"Where's Charlie?" asked Jessi.

"Who knows?" I said. "He was supposed to drive us here but he never showed up. Watson brought us."

"The three of us can run the Klinic ourselves," Jessi reassured me.

Mallory turned green. *"Three of us?"*

"If you don't know what to do," Jessi said, "just ask Kristy."

Jordan raced to us, breathless. "Where's Charlie?"

"He'll be here any minute," Jessi said.

"He's not here yet, guys!" Jordan shouted, running off.

He might as well have said, "Time to goof off!" Rounding up the kids was like trying to corral wild horses. Just as we'd pair them into games of catch, other kids would show up —

and then the practice would fall apart again.

Jessi, Mallory, and I must have heard the question "Where's Charlie?" a million times.

One of those questions was from the Hsus' pretty baby-sitter. It was followed by the question, "And *who* is he?" She was talking to Jessi, and even though I was clear across the field at the time, I could see that look of longing in the girl's eye.

"Well, he's Kristy's brother," Jessi replied. "And she says he'll be here soon."

The girl glanced in my direction with a big smile. (Right. *Now* she noticed me.) "They're related?"

Duh.

Jessi introduced herself and patiently told the sitter our names.

"I'm Angelica," the girl said. "I'll be sitting for the Hsus a lot this vacation."

(Angelica. I knew it was something like that.)

"Great," Jessi said.

Angelica nodded. "I can see the resemblance. Between Kristy and Charlie."

They chatted for awhile. Angelica seemed pretty friendly. Considerate. Funny. (Talkative, too. At the time, I really needed Jessi on the field.)

RRRRRUMMMM-PUTT-PUTT-PUTT . . . BANG!

Their conversation was cut short by a noise that Jessi knew well. The mating call of the Junk Bucket.

That's the name of Charlie's car. It looks like a rusted tin can and it sounds like bronchitis on wheels.

The car sputtered and wheezed to a stop at the curb. The kids all ran to it.

"Cool car," Angelica said, giggling.

Charlie emerged with a huge smile.

And a haircut.

And some new clothes.

I was stunned. The last time my brother actually bought clothes, my mom practically had to drag him to the store by the collar.

The kids were chattering away, yanking on his shirt. Jessi heard Claire say, "P.U.! You stink!"

"Ohhhh, you'll suffer for that!" Charlie cried out, running after her.

Claire squealed with delight as Charlie chased her around. That was when Jessi caught a very strong whiff of something unexpected.

Cologne.

As Charlie released Claire and bounded onto the field, he winked in Jessi's direction.

Jessi knew the wink wasn't for her. And judging by the redness of Angelica's face, *she* knew it, too.

CHAPTER 6

"Charlie's Champs," I said. "That's what they should be called."

Claudia tossed me a bag of licorice strings. "Try some of these. They'll calm your nerves."

"Charlie's Chosen," I mumbled, digging my hand into the bag. "Charlie's Chattering Chimpanzees."

"Kristy," Mallory said, "they're still the Krushers. They're just excited about having a high school kid as a coach."

"Charlie's Angels," I decided. "There we go. Why not fit Angelique's name in there?"

"Angelica," Jessi corrected me.

"Whatever," I grunted.

Claudia's clock read 5:39. We still hadn't had one baby-sitting phone call, which didn't help my rotten mood.

Why was it so rotten? Well, we'd just had Day Three of the so-called Krusher Klinic. Once again, my big brother had shown up smelling like a spice basket. The Hsus' baby-sitter reeked of some floral perfume. I felt as if I'd wandered into a botanical garden. What was worse, Charlie couldn't stop showing off. He wore this T-shirt with rolled-up sleeves so he could display his biceps. Then he broke one of my bats, trying to show how far he could hit.

I mean, really, is that the way to run a serious practice?

It was bad enough that my own team wasn't listening to me. It was bad enough that I was going to have to buy new equipment. But I could deal with both of those things, as long as the players were happy.

If I wanted to watch a love story, though, I could rent a video.

One thing I do know: Sarah, Charlie's old girlfriend, would never have worn perfume to a practice. Or made googly eyes at Charlie. Or offered him a cigarette. (Yes, she smoked. Gross.)

I was beginning to miss Sarah more and more.

"Lo-o-o-ove is idd the airrrr," Abby warbled, her voice clogged with allergies.

"Puh-leeze," I said. "My clinic is turning into a . . . a public date!"

"They weren't that bad," Jessi insisted. "The kids didn't seem to notice. They played pretty well."

I nodded. "Sure. They listen to Charlie even when he's distracted. What do they need me for?"

"Kristyyy . . ." Mary Anne said warningly.

"I mean, why doesn't he just ask her out and get it over with?" I barreled on. "They can dump cologne on themselves, go on a date, smoke cigarettes, and stink up the whole town."

"Why are you so grumpy?" Stacey asked. "So your brother likes this girl. Is that a crime?"

"She seems nice," Jessi said.

"He's just acting so weird," I replied. "He *never* rolled up the sleeves of his T-shirt when he was going out with Sarah. I bought him a bottle of cologne for his birthday last year and he used it as a doorstop. He was normal with Sarah. Totally himself. Now look at him."

"Boys mature slower than girls," Claudia said, wrapping a licorice string around a pretzel. "Everybody knows that."

"Tell it to Angelica," I grumbled. "Maybe Sarah can give her lessons."

"Sounds like you miss Sarah," Mary Anne said.

I took a deep breath. "Yeah. She was cool. She actually liked baseball."

"Give Angelica a chance," Stacey spoke up. "Maybe she's just as nice."

"She seems to know the basic softball rules," Mallory added.

"Really?" I said. "She hasn't said a word to me."

"Aha!" Claudia laughed. "*Now* we know the reason you don't like her!"

"I dod't doe why you guys are baking such a big deal out of this," Abby said. "They're just flirtigg a little."

Rrrrrring!

Claudia snatched up the phone. "Hello, Baby-sitters Club. . . . Hi, Mrs. DeWitt. . . . What? . . . Someone to *bring* Buddy and Suzi to Krusher Klinic on Wednesday? Okay, I'll see what we can do and call you back . . ."

Mary Anne scanned the calendar. "Abby's available."

"It's a deal," Abby said.

We swung into baby-sitting mode, but I wasn't really paying attention. My thoughts were swirling around.

Abby was right. I was making a big deal out of nothing. Angelica seemed okay, but she was no Sarah. That was clear. If I could see that, so could Charlie.

Maybe he wasn't as stupid as I thought he was.

I didn't mention a thing to Charlie when he picked up Abby and me from the meeting. I just couldn't find the words.

We piled silently into the Junk Bucket. Charlie was tapping happily on the steering wheel to the beat of a Blade ballad, "Another Girl," that was blasting from his radio. (Appropriate title, I thought.)

The car had that syrupy sweet smell of old cologne. I almost gagged. Abby and I gave each other a Look and tried not to crack up.

As Charlie pulled away from the curb, he started singing along with the radio: "Ohhhhh, I ammm the remaaaains of a lo-o-o-ove that tiiime forgot . . ."

I don't know how we made it home without barfing. Charlie's voice sounds like the cry of a dying moose. When the Junk Bucket stopped in front of our house, Abby nearly sprinted home.

"What's her hurry?" Charlie asked.

"Allergies," I said. *To your singing*, I wanted to add.

We climbed out of the car and walked toward the back of the house. "Did you decide who you're going to take to the concert?" Charlie asked.

"Claudia," I said. "And you?"

Sarah . . . Sarah . . . Sarah . . . I hoped.

"Probably Travis," Charlie replied. "He likes Blade."

We entered the kitchen through the back

door. The smell of roast beef blasted us and I practically started to drool.

Boy, was I hungry. I must have eaten half a cow during dinner. Not to mention about five biscuits. I was partway through my ice-cream dessert when I remembered about the broken bat.

I glanced at the stove clock. It read 6:37. The sporting goods store downtown would be closing in a few minutes. I'd have to go all the way to the Washington Mall if I wanted to replace it that evening.

"Can someone drive me to Sportworld?" I asked.

"Not me," Charlie said. "I told Travis I'd hang with him after dinner."

"You're the one who broke the bat," I reminded him.

"Send me the bill," Charlie suggested.

Good old Watson ended up taking me. Just outside Sportworld, he ducked into the gourmet food shop next door. (Watson is not an athlete.)

Sportworld has a great selection of wooden bats, but I bought a metal one, just in case Charlie decided to show off again.

Mission accomplished. Clutching my bat, I headed for the gourmet store.

"Kristy . . . hi!" called a familiar voice.

Through the front door of the gourmet store

walked Sarah Green. She was with her mom, and both of them were smiling.

"Hi, Sarah," I said. "Charlie's not here." (Ugh. The words just flew out. I couldn't stop them. I felt like such a goon.)

"How's he doing?" Sarah asked.

"Fine, I guess," I replied. "You know, looking at colleges, whatever. It's kind of confusing."

Sarah nodded. "I know. All those brochures are driving me crazy. Well, tell him I said hi."

"Really? I mean, sure, I will. He'd like that. A lot."

Sarah's face brightened at that. (Okay, maybe it was just wishful thinking, but it sure seemed that way.) "Great. See you soon."

"Good-bye, Kristy," said Mrs. Green.

" 'Bye!" I replied.

See? Even her mom is nice.

Angelica, Shmangelica. Charlie was a total fool to break up with Sarah.

As I walked into the store, I could see Watson at the cheese counter, talking with a clerk.

I waited by the cashier. My mind was racing into Idea Mode. Sarah still liked Charlie. That was clear. Charlie and Angelica had barely even spoken to each other yet.

There was still a chance.

Okay, maybe Charlie and Sarah had fought. Big deal. Why should he lose a great girlfriend over that? Why chase after some strange new girl? Why waste his time? Why waste Krusher Klinic time?

I was going to bring Sarah back into his life, or my name wasn't Kristy the Matchmaker Thomas.

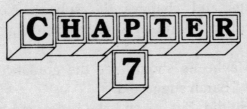

CHAPTER 7

"Hello, Green residence."

I nearly hung up. I'd spent half an hour working up the nerve to call Sarah, and now, at the moment of truth, I felt as if I'd swallowed sandpaper.

I glanced up at the basement door. It was closed. I could hear my family bouncing around upstairs. Shannon was barking gleefully. No one would hear me.

"May I speak to Sarah, please?" I squeaked.

"This is Sarah."

Steady, Thomas, I said to myself. *It'll work. Just say it.*

"Hi, Sarah," I began. "This is Kristy Thomas. It was great to see you tonight at the mall. I was thinking about our conversation, and I wanted to ask you a question."

"Sure."

"Well, it's about colleges. Charlie's totally mixed up. He has about a zillion brochures and they all look the same. Mom and Watson keep telling him to narrow the choices down. They ask him what he's interested in, what kind of job he wants. Does he know? No way. He just shrugs and changes the subject. Now my parents are kind of angry, which makes him angry."

"Maybe he should see the guidance counselor," Sarah suggested.

"He did, but he said she just asked him the same dumb questions. She's so busy she barely knows who he is. Anyway, I was asking myself: Who knows Charlie really, really well? I mean, not a grown-up, but a kid his own age who knows the things he likes in school. And then you popped into my mind."

"Kristy, um, you know that Charlie and I broke up — "

"Sure, sure. Maybe just you and I could meet. I'll sneak you Charlie's college brochures, and you can tell me what's good."

"But I don't know much about colleges — "

"Charlie always talked about how smart and organized you are. Just a few minutes, that's all. Can we meet at the Argo tomorrow at, say, one o'clock? We'll have lunch. I'll treat."

"Well . . ."

"Great! I knew you would, Sarah. This will be very important to my brother. Thanks. 'Bye!"

Bingo.

As I hung up, I murmured, "Yyyyyesss."

Now for Phase Two.

I walked all the way upstairs to the second floor. Charlie's bedroom door was ajar. He was at his desk, playing a computer game. On his screen, spaceships were bombing each other to smithereens.

I poked my head in. "Hey, Coach. Good practice today."

Click-click-click, went Charlie's fingers on the mouse.

BOOOOOM! went the computer.

Charlie punched his fist in the air. *"Got you, you nerd!"*

"Anyway," I said loudly, "I really appreciate your help. A lot. You know, I was thinking: How can I possibly repay my brother?"

Click-click-click-click. "You don't have to."

"How about having lunch at the Argo to-morrow, right after practice?"

Charlie finally put the game on pause and turned around. "You're my little sister. What if someone sees me?"

I picked up a sock from his floor and threw it at him. "Ha-ha. Look, I'm treating."

"How'd *you* get so rich?"

"I save my allowance instead of spending it on dumb computer games."

Charlie aimed the mouse at me and clicked

it. "You're asteroid dust. And you pay for everything tomorrow."

"Okay. See you."

I practically skipped to my room.

Kristy, you are a genius, I said to myself.

It was going to work. I knew it.

At Klinic the next day, I couldn't concentrate.

Big Ideas are funny. Each one seems to change with time. Sometimes it just seems smarter and smarter. Sometimes you begin to wonder if you'd lost your mind when you thought of it.

This one was closer to the lost-your-mind variety.

The idea had seemed perfect the night before. Charlie would see Sarah, Sarah would see Charlie, they'd both realize it was dumb to break up. Happy ending.

But the more I thought about it, the stupider it seemed. What if it was too soon to bring them together? What if Charlie and Sarah really were sick of each other? What if they became angry at me for setting them up? They might order from the dinner menu and make me pay. They might throw sugar canisters at me.

I could always wear a batting helmet. . . .

I tried to put these thoughts out of my mind.

It was Day Four of the Klinic, and we had lots of work.

How did my Krushers do? Pretty well, considering that the Papadakis and Barrett kids both had to miss the practice because of family commitments. For the first time all week, Jamie Newton did not run away when a ball was thrown to him. Jackie made it through the practice without injuring anyone. Claire managed to swing the bat without falling down. Charlie and Angelica seemed to be easing up on the cologne.

Progress.

When it was over, David Michael, Charlie, and I piled into the front seat of the Junk Bucket.

"Uh, we don't have to squeeze, David Michael," I said. "The Papadakises aren't here."

"I want to ride up front!" David Michael insisted.

Charlie leaned out the open window and called out: "Hey, guys! We have some space. Want a ride?"

I looked outside to see Angelica and the Hsu kids running toward the car.

Oh, groan.

The three of them scrambled into the backseat. Angelica must have thanked Charlie a million times. She kept thanking him even after he started driving. Charlie didn't even grow sick of it. He kept saying "You're welcome" and "Hey, my pleasure," as if he'd just given Angelica a winning lottery ticket.

I was so happy when we finally dropped them off in front of the Hsus'.

"Well, thanks," Angelica said (again) as she climbed out.

"Wait!" Charlie blurted out. "Kristy and I are going to the Argo for lunch. Want to come?"

Clunk. My jaw hit the floor of the car.

David Michael was jumping up and down on the seat. "If Timmy and Scott are going, I want to go, too!"

"No!" I almost shouted. "I mean, *no* children are allowed."

Charlie gave me a funny look. "Kids eat in there all the time."

"Uh . . . well, I only have enough money for two."

"I have cash," Charlie said.

"Me, too," Angelica added. "I'll just drop off the kids and meet you in front of your house!"

"Ohhhhhhh," groaned David Michael, Timmy, and Scott.

Angelica laughed sweetly. "Come on, guys."

As Angelica and the Hsus walked toward the house, Charlie zoomed away from the curb.

"You can't!" I blurted out. "I mean, she can't

come, Charlie. This was supposed to be just for me and you!"

"I see you every day, Kristy. What's the big deal? Besides, you want to thank me for coaching, right? Well, think of Angelica. She's been here every day helping the kids, too."

"But not with baseball! She's a sitter, Charlie. I'm not inviting the other sitters, am I?"

Charlie stopped in front of our house. "All seven-year-old sluggers out!"

"Unfair," David Michael mumbled as he opened the door and skulked away.

"That's it, it's unfair!" I said. "I mean, here I am, going out of my way. Offering to take you out. And you're — you're making it seem like, la-di-da, let's invite just anyone."

Charlie rolled his eyes. "Okay, okay, fine."

I could see Angelica running toward us now. Her hair was flowing behind her, her teeth gleaming in the sun. She looked like a toothpaste commercial.

I wished I had a remote so I could zap to the next channel.

"Hi!" Angelica said, reaching for the door handle.

"Uh, Angelica," Charlie said. "I'm really sorry, but my sister says this was supposed to be some kind of private lunch. She's, like, angry at me for inviting you — "

"I'm not angry!" I said. "It's just that I

wanted to thank my brother personally."

"Oh." Angelica nodded. "That's nice. I wish my sister would do something like that."

"Maybe tomorrow?" Charlie said. "Just, you know, me and you?"

Bing! Back came the toothpaste smile. "Sure!"

She backed away, and Charlie started away from the curb. " 'Bye!" he called out. "Sorry!"

I flopped back into my seat. Boy, was I relieved.

I also felt like a total jerk. "Don't be mad at me, okay?"

"Sure, Kristy."

Just hang on, I wanted to tell him. *You'll be glad I did this.*

As Charlie drove into the Argo parking lot, I saw Sarah's bike in the rack. Fortunately, Charlie didn't seem to notice it.

We parked, then walked into the restaurant. My heart was thumping so hard, it felt as if I'd swallowed a jackhammer.

"Table for two?" asked a waitress.

"Kristy, over here!" Sarah's voice called out from my left.

I turned. Sarah rose from a nearby table, smiling.

The smile lasted about a nanosecond. She suddenly looked as if someone had erased the color from her face.

"Charlie?" she said.

"Uh — uh — " Charlie stuttered.

"I have to go to the bathroom," I quickly said.

Zoom.

The next time I exhaled, I was standing over the sink. I took a lo-o-o-ong time washing my hands. I counted silently to 257. I thought about something Dawn Schafer once told me: If you want something badly, you visualize it clearly in your mind until it seems you can see it. You can actually will it to become real.

I closed my eyes and visualized Charlie and Sarah, sitting at a table, sharing a laugh, holding hands. Thanking me, with tears of joy running down their cheeks.

Then a customer knocked at the door, so I had to leave.

Sarah was sitting at the table, glumly toying with the utensils. Charlie was standing on the other side of the table, looking at his feet.

As I approached, he looked up. His eyes were not twinkly.

"Well, guys," I said, "I guess I'd better leave you two alone. I can walk — "

"I'll drive you," Charlie interrupted. "I forgot, I was supposed to play basketball with Travis."

I glanced at Sarah. "But what about — ?" I began.

"That's all right," Sarah said. "I couldn't stay long anyway."

"Okay, 'bye," Charlie said. He was out the door like a shot.

"But — but — " I sputtered.

I looked at Sarah. If eyes were spears, I'd be human shish kebab.

If I hadn't run to the Junk Bucket, I think Charlie would have driven off without me. He tore out of the parking lot and lurched onto the street. We were quiet for a few minutes.

My heart was down around my instep. "Charlie," I said, "I can explain . . ."

Charlie yanked the steering wheel hard onto McLelland Road. I nearly barfed. "You think I'm stupid?" he snapped. "You think I don't know what that was all about?"

"Okay, it was dumb, but — "

"Typical! Typical Sarah Green. She set this up, didn't she? She used you, Kristy. And you fell for it!"

"*Whaaaat?* That wasn't it at all — "

"If she wanted to talk to me, couldn't she just call? She had to pull something like this?"

"She didn't pull anything! I — "

"I'm sorry I ever went out with her!" Charlie skidded to a stop in front of the house. "See you later, Kristy. I'm taking a drive."

"But Charlie, it wasn't Sarah — "

"Just go, okay? I don't want to talk about it."

It was no use. Charlie wasn't listening. I stepped out of the car.

The moment the door shut, he was off.

I felt about two inches tall.

CHAPTER 8

Wednesday

Well, it was a
hap-hap-happy
day at the Krusher
Klinic. The weather
was fair, the humor
foul. Some of the
behavior was out
of left field. We
batted around a
few ideas, and a
few of them
caught on. And
I took lots of
pitchers before I
went home....

That's Abby. When things go wrong, she tells jokes. The worse the better.

Fortunately, she's a good athlete. Which makes the humor less painful.

Abby and Mrs. DeWitt had brought Buddy and Suzi Barrett and the Kuhn kids to the Krusher Klinic on Wednesday. And boy, was I glad to see her. Jokes or not.

Charlie wasn't talking to me. It was the day after the Argo disaster, and yes, I'd finally told him the truth about what I'd done.

I'd also told Abby. She could feel the chill between Charlie and me. She was going overboard to make everyone laugh. The whole team had shown up, so she had a big audience.

I was playing catch with David Michael, beyond the first-base foul line. Charlie was on the opposite side of the diamond, hitting soft grounders to some of the Pike kids while flirting with Angelica. Abby was in the middle, coaching Claire at home plate.

Poor Claire. Because she's so little, she usually brings her own bat. But she'd forgotten it, so now she was struggling with the new metal one. It seemed to be swinging *her*.

"Choke up on it, Claire," Abby said. "Like this."

She took the bat from Claire. Then Abby assumed a batting stance, her hands way up toward the thick part.

"Let me try," Claire said, taking the bat.

Thunk. Claire hit the ball off the tee. It rolled slowly toward the middle of the infield.

"Good one, Claire!" Abby cried out.

"Yeeeeaaaa!" screamed Claire.

Behind second base, Scott Hsu stuck out his glove and squatted. The ball came to a stop about fifteen feet in front of him. Scott stood where he was, looking a little puzzled.

"Run in for it!" Abby called out.

All the infielders — Hannie, Scott, Timmy, Suzi, and Patsy — sprinted toward the ball.

Abby decided to teach them a lesson. She ran to first. "Uh-oh, here goes the runner! Who's covering first base?"

Hannie threw the ball to the empty, player-less space above first. It rolled into foul territory.

Abby kept running. "I'm stealing second!" she shouted, lifting the base off the dirt and tucking it under her arms.

The kids were running around like crazy, chasing after the ball and throwing it to no one in particular.

When Abby reached home, she held second base, third base, and home plate triumphantly over her head. "Three stolen bases!"

The kids were cracking up. Linny Papadakis had snatched first base and put it on his head.

Charlie did not find this funny. He trotted over to Abby and said, "You know, we're supposed to set an example! This is softball, not play-with-the-bases."

"I'm just trying to teach them a lesson and make it fun," Abby said.

"Okay, team!" Charlie shouted. "We're going to split in half again and play a practice inning. Anyone who lifts a base is an automatic out!"

"Party pooper," Abby muttered.

"What?" Charlie asked.

"Sounds super," Abby said quickly.

"But I want to bat some more!" Claire complained.

"You'll get your chance," Charlie said. "Everyone over here — now!"

Out went Claire's lower lip.

I was fed up with Charlie's bullying. I stomped down the first-base line toward him. "Abby was in the middle of batting practice, Charlie."

Charlie glared at me. "So?"

"So? You're not the only coach here."

"Okay, fine. You're the boss. Maybe you don't need my help anymore."

"I didn't say that, Charlie — "

"You know, I don't *have* to be here," Charlie

retorted. "If it weren't for the kids, I might not be. I didn't think I'd spend my vacation being used by my sister."

Scream. Yell. Bop him over the head with home plate. That's what I wanted to do.

But I choked it all back. I did not want the Krushers to see their coaches fighting. Besides, Charlie was right. Sort of.

"Go ahead, but please let Claire bat first," I said patiently, then stormed away to the bench.

Abby piped up, "All kids with vowels in their names, to my right. All kids with consonants in their names, to my left!"

"What if you have both?" asked Jackie.

The kids were running around, bumping into each other, giggling.

Angelica began laughing. Then Charlie did, too.

Me? At that moment, I didn't find anything very funny.

Soon Charlie began barking instructions, and the kids all jumped to it. Good old Abby was making jokes, trying her hardest to keep everyone happy.

One coach for discipline, one for fun. My team had everything it needed. Boy, did I feel unnecessary.

I could not look at Charlie. Angelica was now standing next to him wherever he went.

They would not stop yammering. I couldn't

hear a word they were saying, but I could tell the topic of conversation was not softball.

Abby, however, was standing near them, and overheard every word they said.

"Your sister looks so upset," Angelica remarked softly.

"Sure," Charlie said with a little snorting laugh. "*You're* here."

"She doesn't like me?" Angelica replied.

"Remember that lunch she took me to yesterday?" Charlie went on. "The special one between her and me, that you couldn't go to? Well, there was a reason she didn't want you there — "

Abby to the rescue. "Uh . . . Charlie! I think we need some outfield coaching. Matt's up."

Matt Braddock is a great hitter, but the outfield was playing way too shallow.

"Back up!" Charlie yelled.

Thump-thump-thump-thump went the players.

Charlie turned to Angelica again. Quickly Abby asked, "So, what'd you think of that Yankees game last night?"

"Didn't see it," Charlie said over his shoulder. "See, she had called my old girlfriend, Sarah . . ."

Abby was cringing. She could see Angelica's face sag as Charlie told her the story of the Argo.

When he finished, Angelica was lighting up

a cigarette and scowling. "Well, do you still, you know, like this girl?"

Charlie laughed. "Nahhh, we broke up. She's okay, though. After Kristy told me the truth, I called her. Just to apologize about being a jerk. I mean, it wasn't her fault. She was cool. We're buds. But that's all."

Charlie put his arm around Angelica, and she snuggled against him.

I mean, really, can you be more obvious?

"Oooooh," said Linny Papadakis.

"Charlie and Angelica, sitting in a tree . . ." Scott began singing.

The kids giggled.

Angelica giggled.

Charlie was too macho to giggle. He laughed heroically.

I forced myself not to barf.

Abby tried desperately to make jokes. And she vowed never to tell me that Charlie had spilled the news to Angelica.

CHAPTER 9

"*H*e *told her what?*"

Flabbergasted. Betrayed. Humiliated. That's how I felt.

Abby did not keep her vow. She waited until Charlie drove us home, then invited me over to her house. We were strolling up her walk when she told me.

"Kristy, I'm sorry," Abby said. "I was going to keep my mouth shut about it. But I thought it wouldn't be fair to you. You needed to know. I didn't mean to upset you."

"Upset? I'm not upset. Why should I care what Angelica knows?"

"Good, I was hoping you'd take it that way."

"Charlie won't talk to me. Sarah won't talk to me. And now Charlie's new girlfriend hates my guts. Upset? Me?"

Abby put her hand on my shoulder. "Come on inside and relax."

Anna's violin playing was echoing through the house. It was some sad classical piece. I felt as if I were in an old black-and-white movie. It didn't do wonders for my mood.

"How dare he?" I said, pacing around the kitchen. "This was between me and him and Sarah!"

Abby brought out a bag of pretzels and a bottle of soda. "Don't take this the wrong way, Kristy, but maybe you should put yourself in his shoes. I mean, what you did was not exactly kosher."

I exhaled hard. "Yeah, I know. It was dumb."

"Hey, once in awhile we all do something really boneheaded. Even the great Kristy Thomas."

"Still, I did apologize to him. He didn't have to spread it around. If you heard him, others must have, too. How am I going to show my face at Klinic again?"

"Try this." Abby crossed her eyes and curled up her lips.

I ignored the joke. "Now she must think I hate her."

"You do hate her."

"I do not! I don't even know her."

"Well, it looks like you probably will, Kristy. You should have heard some of the other gooshy stuff they were saying to each other."

"I noticed. He was more interested in her than the players."

"That's all right. I kept them busy."

"But what about when you're away, Abby? He's supposed to help me. I mean, my brother's love life is his business, but when he's at the Krusher Klinic, he's on Krusher time."

"Tell him that, Kristy."

"It's not so easy. He's doing me a favor. I'm lucky he's still showing up. If I make him even angrier, he'll quit. I'll be stranded."

Abby nodded. "Listen, Kristy, whatever you do, don't tell him I told you what I heard. Then he'll know that I know that Angelica knows about what you did at the Argo."

I took a deep breath. "Yeah, okay. I won't."

I felt trapped. I couldn't tell anyone anything.

Did I deserve this? I'd tried to do the right thing. I'd tried to do something nice for my brother. Something that would make him happy. Okay, maybe it wasn't the smartest way to do it, but the intention was good.

The whole thing had blown up in my face.

I should have minded my own business. I should have just left well enough alone and concentrated on running the softball clinic. Even that was slipping out of my hands. My players didn't know I existed.

How did everything become so complicated?

"Some spring break," I muttered.

I stayed at Abby's the rest of the afternoon. She tried so hard to make me feel better. She convinced Anna to play me some fiddle music she'd learned. That was cool. Then Abby called Claudia and invited her over. Claudia brought a new outfit she'd put together for the Blade concert. Abby and Anna oohed and aahed over it. (To me, it looked like something Cinderella might have thrown out — although I didn't tell Claudia that.)

Claudia offered to take me shopping for the concert. I said no way, José.

We then rushed over to Claud's house for a BSC meeting. By the time I went home for dinner, my mood had lifted a little. As I walked up the front lawn, the Junk Bucket was pulling out of the driveway.

Mom was on the porch, waving to Charlie.

"Where's he going?" I asked.

"Out on a date," Mom replied with a smile. "Some new girlfriend."

"Cool," I said.

I walked inside. I went straight to the kitchen. Calmly, coolly, I helped prepare dinner.

I was determined not to be upset about anything. Okay, so now Charlie was dating

Angelica. It was official. Sarah was a thing of the past. No big surprise.

It was my brother's life. Not my concern.

From now on, I was going to mind my own business.

Late that night the sound of the Junk Bucket awoke me from my sleep. I heard the engine sputter and stop. A few minutes later I caught a whiff of Charlie's cologne wafting upstairs and heard Mom's footsteps trudging downstairs.

They managed to keep their argument pretty soft, although I did hear Charlie say, "But the movie didn't end until midnight!"

I smiled. Let Charlie get into trouble for a change.

I fell asleep again and didn't awaken until my alarm went off at eight in the morning. I'd scheduled Krusher Klinic for nine-thirty that day, and David Michael was still snoozing away. I practically had to carry him downstairs to breakfast.

The kitchen rang out with a chorus of good mornings. Nannie was feeding Emily. I could hear Sam singing in the downstairs shower.

Charlie was deep in conversation on the kitchen phone. As I went to the cereal cupboard, I heard him hang up and shout, "Yyyyesss!"

"What's up?" I asked.

He was racing to the back door. "You'll find out."

"Where are you going?"

"Having breakfast with a friend."

Uh-huh. Right.

"Breakfast, too?" I said. "Why don't you just move in with her family?"

"Kristyyyy," Nannie said.

"Whose family?" David Michael asked.

"Never mind!" Charlie gave me a sharp look, then raced toward the door. "See you at Klinic."

"Wait!" I said. "How are we supposed to get there?"

"Can you drive them, Nannie?" Charlie shouted over his shoulder.

"I can," Nannie said. "And I think I may."

David Michael and I wolfed down breakfast. When Nannie was ready, she drove us to SES.

We arrived way early, but guess what? About half the team was already there, playing catch with their parents and sitters. They were all laughing and having a great time.

"Good team spirit," Nannie remarked as David Michael and I stepped out.

"The Klinic has really helped," I replied. "Thanks for the ride, Nannie."

Walking onto the field, I breathed in the

sweet smell of new-mown grass. The sun warmed my face, and the breeze was so cool and fresh I felt I could drink it.

Mr. Pike was smacking grounders. The Krusher infielders were eagerly chasing the ball (even fielding it occasionally).

I could not help grinning. This — this was how the Klinic was supposed to be. Good energy, hard work, fun. A foolproof winning formula.

Bart's Bashers, be prepared.

"Way to go, guys!" I called out.

By nine-thirty, Charlie still hadn't shown. Neither had the Hsu boys or Angelica (surprise, surprise). I started the practice anyway. Completely solo.

You know what? I didn't mind at all. It felt great to be number one again.

"Okay, everybody in the outfield!" I called out. "Jumping jacks!"

I love doing calisthenics with the kids. They think it's so funny. They dance around like monkeys. Their sit-ups and push-ups are hilarious. Why do I make them do it? For team spirit. They loosen up and start off the practice eager and happy.

That, to me, is what good coaching is all about.

We were halfway through a base-running

drill when the Hsu kids ran onto the field. Angelica and Charlie were trotting along behind them.

"Sorry!" Angelica called out. "We burned some of the pancake batter."

She nudged Charlie in the ribs. He smiled in an *aw-shucks-it-was-my-fault* way.

Oh, groan.

"Okay, team, let's split up!" I cried out. "We need to concentrate on fly balls — "

"Hold it!" Charlie interrupted. "I need the whole team here, front and center!"

Forget about fly balls. The kids were around Charlie in a second.

His face was flushed with excitement. "I have fantastic news. How many of you know who Jack Brewster is?"

About half the kids nodded.

"Hall of Famer for the Mets!" Jake said.

"Right," Charlie replied. "And he is going to be our guest coach the day after tomorrow!"

This was news to me.

"*YEAAAAAA!*" The Krushers were jumping all over each other with excitement.

"We need to show him how good we are," Charlie said, "so let's hit the field and practice!"

The kids ran back into position. Kindly but firmly, I asked Charlie, "Why didn't you tell me?"

"I only found out this morning," Charlie said with a shrug. "And I wanted it to be a surprise."

With that, he strolled back to the stands, where Angelica was sitting.

I ran the fly ball practice. I hit more grounders. I gave lots of individual tips.

Where was Charlie while this was going on? Guess. Four times I had to call him onto the field. Four times he helped out a little, barking out commands. Then — *zzzzzip!* — back to his number-one fan.

Soon the kids were looking sharp. They were ready for a few practice innings, so I organized teams.

"Okay, I'll be behind first," I announced, "and Charlie will umpire — "

I looked toward the stands. Charlie wasn't there.

"Charlie?" I called out.

"There he is!" said Suzi Barrett, pointing toward the school playground.

There, inside the chain-link fence, Charlie and Angelica were soaring up and down on the swings.

"Charlieeeee!" I shouted.

He waved. He stopped pumping his legs.

I turned back to the game. "Let's start without him," I grumbled.

Suzi was up first and hit a single. Then Matt

hit a triple, sending her home. The third batter was Laurel. She hit a slow grounder to the pitcher's area.

Linny raced in and tossed it to first. Buddy caught it just as Laurel stepped on the base.

"Out!" Buddy called.

"Safe!" Laurel said.

"Kristyyyyyyyy, what was it?" Buddy cried out.

The truth? I hadn't seen. I'd been blocked by the catcher. Charlie was supposed to be the ump.

I glanced toward the playground. Now the swings were empty. In the distance, just beyond the school, I spotted two familiar figures, strolling arm in arm.

About ten players had crowded around first base, crying "Out!" and "Safe!" at the top of their lungs.

"Time out!" I yelled as I ran to Mrs. DeWitt. "Would you keep an eye on them for a minute while I go get my brother?"

She agreed, and I sprinted away.

Charlie and Angelica were in mid-laugh when I reached them. As if they had all the time in the world. "Uh, excuse me!" I called out. "Where are you going?"

Charlie glanced at me, then looked at Angelica and rolled his eyes. "For a walk, Kristy."

As if I were a nincompoop. An annoying,

dumb, bossy little nincompoop sister.

My blood was boiling. "In case you forgot, the clinic is behind you."

"You seem to be doing fine, Kristy," Charlie said.

"So you can just wander away without saying anything? You can simply walk in, tell everybody about Jack Brewster, be a big hero, and then abandon your team?"

"Will you lighten up, Kristy? I'm not *abandoning* it. Look, I agreed to *help* you. Haven't I been doing that?"

"But you're the official co-coach."

"I don't have a contract. I'm free to do whatever I want — "

"*That* sounds familiar," I shot back. "I guess it runs in the family, huh? Now that you're so grown up, you can act just like Dad?"

Charlie spun around. He looked flabbergasted. "I can't believe you said that, Kristy."

"Sometimes the truth hurts," I replied, storming back to the field.

CHAPTER 10

Friday

Today I sat for Jamie Newton. He was very excited about the Klinic. On the walk there, he could not stop talking about Jake Broneton, or whatever his name is. He kept asking me baseball questions, too. I tried to explain that I knew nothing about baseball.

Then, when Kristy announced that I was going to co-coach, Jamie was ecstatic. Me? I nearly died....

Mary Anne is to sports what I am to high fashion.

She never goes near the stuff.

Normally she'd be the last person I'd ask to coach. But I was desperate. Klinic was about to start, and Charlie was nowhere to be seen. That morning he'd stomped out of the house without saying a word. He hadn't spoken to me since our argument, almost a whole day earlier.

Poor Mary Anne. She wasn't suspecting a thing. As she walked onto the field with Jamie, she was clutching a paperback book, looking forward to a nice, quiet morning of reading.

"So the ball was coming to me like this: *nyeeeeeeeeeaar* . . ." Jamie said, imitating the flight of the ball with one arm. "And I went like this." He backpedaled, waving his arms. "And the ball went like this — pop!" He acted out a dramatic catch.

Mary Anne nodded patiently. "Uh-huh . . . wow."

"Mary Anne!" I said, running to her. "Charlie's not here yet. Can you hit some grounders?"

You should have seen her face. It was as if I'd asked her to cut down a tree with her teeth. "Well, uh, sure, I guess, but — "

"Thanks," I said, turning back to the practice. "You're a great pal."

"Wait, Kristy!" Mary Anne called out. "One question. What are they?"

"What are what?"

"Grounders."

Hoo, boy. "Ground balls. You know, you hit them? I'll set up the tee. It'll be easy."

Jamie was now reenacting his catch for a small audience of Krusher fielders. I fetched Mary Anne a bat, then put the tee at home plate. Mary Anne stepped up to the right side of the plate cautiously, as if it were the hole at the top of a volcano.

"You bat lefty?" I asked.

"Huh?"

"Where you're standing. That's where a left-handed batter would stand."

"Oh. I guess I'm wrong." Mary Anne shuffled around to the other side of the plate. "Now, I just . . . swing?"

I put the ball on the tee. "Give it a whack. For practice."

"Hit it to me!" cried three or four voices in the outfield.

Mary Anne swallowed hard. She drew back the bat, closed her eyes, and swung.

She connected with a solid thud — in the middle of the tee. It flopped over onto the ground.

The kids cracked up. Mary Anne's face grew bright red.

86

"Try again," I said.

On the third try, Mary Anne managed to hit the ball. Well, *hit* might be too strong a word. *Brush against* was more like it. The ball fell off the tee and dribbled a few feet.

"This is ridiculous, Kristy," Mary Anne said.

"You're doing great," I lied. "Keep it up. Everyone has to start somewhere. Besides, it's just temporary, until Charlie comes."

I ran off to work with the littlest Krushers.

"Here, Mary Anne! Here!" shouted Karen from shortstop position.

"Uh, okay," Mary Anne said.

She swung the bat clear over the top of the ball. Then she pulled the bat back to try again.

Whack! The ball shot backward. It smacked against the fence behind home plate.

"Hoooo-hahahaha!" howled Linny from first base.

Mary Anne turned to retrieve the ball. She heard the Junk Bucket pull up to the curb, and she thought: *rescue!*

Charlie climbed out and jogged toward the field. Behind him, Angelica was helping Timmy and Scott out.

"Hi!" Mary Anne called out. "Want to hit some grinders?"

"Grounders," Charlie said, taking the bat. "Would you do me a favor, Mary Anne?"

"Sure." Mary Anne was so happy to be bat-less, she probably would have done a tap dance if he'd asked.

"Would you ask my sister if I'm still going to the concert tonight? Or was she so mad at me she gave the tickets away?"

"I'll ask," Mary Anne said uncertainly.

As she walked toward me. Charlie stepped to the plate. "Okay, all you golden gloves! Show me how you're going to impress Jack Brewster!"

SMACK!

The sound of Charlie's sharp grounders echoed off the school walls. I saw him, but I wasn't paying much attention. I mean, if Charlie wasn't going to say hi to me, I wasn't going to go out of my way, either. Besides, I was teaching Nina Marshall how to catch. Nina's four, and she was just starting to get the hang of it.

"Excuse me, Kristy," Mary Anne said. "Charlie wants to know if he's going to the concert, or if you gave his tickets away."

I turned away from Nina. "Suddenly he can't trust me ever again? Tell him I wouldn't just give the tickets away to someone else without telling him. Even though I probably should."

Mary Anne jogged back to Charlie. "She says yes, you're going."

"Great," Charlie said, glancing my way.

"Now, would you tell her I won't be going home after Klinic, so don't freak out. I'll be home later, for dinner, and I'll drive to the concert."

Across the field again went Mary Anne the Messenger. Once again she told me Charlie's message.

"Mary Anne, you shouldn't be running over here like his slave," I said. "Anyway, ask him if we're going to pick up Travis, and if we are, tell him we have to leave early. And tell him that Claudia needs a ride, too."

"Can I ask you something?" Mary Anne asked.

"What?"

"Why don't you just talk to him?"

"Why should I, if he can't talk to me? You can tell him I said that. And you can say you refuse to trot back here again. If he wants to say something to me, he can do it himself!"

"Okay, Kristy."

Mary Anne was beginning to feel like a tennis ball.

She asked Charlie about Travis and told him about Claudia. Then she quickly added, "And Kristy said she'd love to talk to you, if you wouldn't mind going over there for a minute."

Charlie gave her the bat. "Smack a few, Mary Anne. I'll be back."

Oh, groan. Mary Anne stood there with the bat, looking at it as if it were a dead eel.

"Um, guys?" she called out. "I'll throw you the grounders instead, okay?"

"Let *me* hit them!" Linny volunteered, running toward the plate.

"You can't do that!" Hannie said. "Your grounders will have cooties."

"Only if you field them," Linny shot back.

Now Buddy was rushing in, too. "Linny always gets to hit! I want to!"

"No, me!"

One by one, the fielders ran toward Mary Anne, flinging their mitts away.

"Wait!" Mary Anne said. "Who's going to field?"

"You!" Linny replied.

Buddy tossed Mary Anne her mitt. "But — but I — " she protested.

Linny was already in batting position at the tee. "Hurry! This is going to the fences!"

Mary Anne turned wearily and jogged into the field.

At the same time, I was running to her with Nina. "Uh, Kristy?" Mary Anne said. "Are the kids allowed to line up for batting with only one fielder — "

"Do you know what my brother just told me?" I said through gritted teeth.

"No, but Linny's about to — "

"He's not taking Travis to the concert," I barreled on. "He's taking *Angelica!* I'm going to have to sit with the love birds for three whole hours!"

WHACK!

A softball soared above our heads. I watched its flight into the empty outfield. *"Who's supposed to be fielding that?"* I bellowed.

I looked at the infield. Linny was circling the bases, pumping his fists. The others were standing in a clump by home plate, screaming and yelling.

When I turned back, Mary Anne was gone. She was trudging after the ball, all alone. Looking as if she couldn't wait to go home.

CHAPTER 11

Charlie cleared his throat. He leaned forward, elbows on the dining room table. "Watson, you're not using your car tonight, are you?"

"Did the Junk Bucket finally break down?" Watson asked.

"Not yet," Charlie replied.

"Flat tire?"

"No."

"Another hole in the muffler?"

"Nope."

"Then why are you asking about my car?"

"He wants to borrow it," David Michael piped up.

Charlie gave him a Look. "The Junk Bucket's great for riding around town. If it breaks down here, no problem. I walk to a repair station. But Stamford's a long trip."

"He just doesn't want to be embarrassed,"

Sam remarked, "riding in that old jalopy with his new *girlfriend*."

"Charlie and Angelica, Charlie and Angelica!" David Michael sang.

Watson raised his eyebrows. "Hmmmm, I don't know, Charlie. *Sarah* never seemed to mind the Junk Bucket."

"That's not the reason!" Charlie said, his face turning red.

Watson looked at his watch. "This is short notice . . ."

"I've been busy," Charlie said.

Busy with Angelica, I wanted to say.

"Well, Kristy and Claudia will be chaperoning you," Watson said with a smile, "so I suppose you can use it. With a few conditions."

"Sure!" Charlie said happily.

"Drive slowly," Watson said.

"Okay."

"Use your signals."

"Okay."

"And load the dishwasher."

I have never seen my brother so eager to do chores. He cleared the table. (He tried to clear my ice-cream bowl before I'd eaten seconds, but I grabbed it back.)

I scarfed down the rest of my Heath Bar Crunch, then ran upstairs. My heart felt like a tomtom. It was beating to the rhythm of the title tune from Blade's new CD, *Shrunken Heads*.

All day long I'd been singing, humming, thinking Blade tunes. Now it was 6:25. In a little more than an hour and a half, I was going to be meeting Blade, live!

I changed from my Krushers sweatshirt and jeans into a Blade sweatshirt and a pair of jeans ripped at the knee. I checked myself in the mirror. Fine. Time to go.

Rrrrrring!

"I'll get it!" I ran into my parents' room and snatched up the phone receiver. "Hello!"

"Eeeeeaaaagh!"

My ear was assaulted by a screaming Kishi.

"Are you ready?" I asked.

"I've been ready for an hour! When are you going to pick me up?"

"We're leaving now!"

"Great! Oh! Remember my black Spandex pants? I'm going to wear them instead of the jeans. I hope that doesn't change your plans."

"Whaaat?"

"Good. Be here in thirty seconds. 'Bye."

" 'Bye."

Honk! Honk!

That was the horn of Watson's car. I bolted downstairs and out of the house, shouting a loud good-bye.

Watson and Mom were waving to us from the front door as we pulled away.

Actually, *lurched* away was more like it. I felt as if I were in a bumper car. "What are you doing, Charlie, trying to activate the air bags?"

"I'm not used to power brakes," he replied.

He turned right at the end of the block, and I slammed against the door. "Owww!"

"Power steering, too," Charlie explained.

I never thought a ride in an Oldsmobile could be so treacherous. By the time we arrived at Angelica's, I was struggling to keep down my Heath Bar Crunch.

"Uh, Kristy, would you mind . . . ?" Charlie was eyeing the backseat in a very obvious way.

Grumbling, I climbed out the front door and into the back.

I was dreading this moment. Angelica and I hadn't said a word to each other since the day Charlie told her about the Argo disaster.

Charlie and Angelica strolled out her front door, arm in arm. Charlie actually held open the passenger door for her. (I had *never* seen him do that before.)

Angelica seemed a little puzzled when she saw me. "Hi. Are we driving you home?"

Charlie zoomed around to the driver's side. "Kristy's coming with us."

"Oh." Angelica smiled tightly.

"You didn't tell her?" I asked Charlie.

Charlie shrugged. "Sorry. I forgot."

"I was the one who won the tickets," I reminded him.

"No problem," Angelica said.

No problem?

Thank you would have been nice. *Congratulations*, even. But *no problem*?

"Everyone belted in?" Charlie asked.

"Yup," Angelica and I replied.

Eeeee, went the tires.

Thump, went Angelica against the car door.

"Sorry," said Charlie.

"Please take it easy," Angelica said. "I get motion sickness."

Charlie turned white.

Heh-heh. Now I was glad to be in the backseat.

We circled around the block and headed for Claudia's neighborhood.

Angelica pointed to the left. "Where are you going? The highway's that way."

"Uh, Claudia Kishi's coming with us, too," Charlie explained.

"Oh?" Now the smile was a thin horizontal line.

When we arrived at Claudia's, she was waiting at the curb. She was wearing fringed jeans.

"What happened to the Spandex?" I asked.

"I thought this would be more *Blade*," Claudia replied, climbing into the backseat with me. "Is this Angelique?"

"Angelica," said Angelica.

"Oops." Claudia giggled. "Just for that, you can call me Claudius."

Angelica kind of nodded and looked straight ahead. I don't think she got the hang of Claudia's humor.

"To Stamford, Charles!" Claudia commanded. "Blade, here we come. I am *so-o-o-o* excited."

Charlie popped a Blade cassette into the car radio. The lead singer, Declan Kelly, began wailing at the top of his lungs.

Eeeeee!

That was the car, not Declan Kelly.

We all slammed against the backs of our seats.

"Uh, don't be too excited," Claudia remarked.

Angelica gestured up ahead. "Charlie, at this stop sign, just ease your foot down slowly, okay?"

"Okay," Charlie murmured.

We jolted forward.

"*At* the stop sign!" Angelica said. "Not half a block away from it."

"Ride 'em, cowboy!" Claudia shouted.

"It's just so *different* from my car," Charlie was muttering. "But I'll get the hang of it."

Fat chance. After five or so blocks, I felt as if I'd been in a Cuisinart.

Angelica was looking grim. "Charlie," she finally said, "how about letting me drive?"

"Huh?" Charlie asked.

My reaction exactly.

"No offense," Angelica said, "but I'm already feeling nauseated and we're not out of Stoneybrook."

"But — but — " Charlie stammered.

"Look, I'm used to this kind of car," Angelica pleaded. "My mom taught me to drive on one just like it."

Charlie was slowing down, steering toward the curb.

I could not believe my eyes.

"Charlie, you can't!" I blurted out. "This is Watson's car, not yours."

"He didn't say no one else could drive it," Charlie protested.

"You didn't ask him!" I said.

"It's okay," Angelica insisted. "The insurance covers other drivers. That's the way insurance works."

She might as well have ended that sentence with the words *little girl.*

Charlie pulled to a stop. He and Angelica climbed out.

"Kristy, relax," Claudia whispered. "She can't be worse than him."

"I don't care! Watson is going to kill him!"

Charlie was glaring at me as he slid into the frontseat. "He doesn't have to know, Kristy."

"Oh, now I'm supposed to keep *your* little embarrassing secret?" I snapped.

"What's that supposed to mean?" said Charlie.

Angelica closed her door and put the car in gear. "Off we go!"

We rolled away from the curb. How was Angelica's driving? Better than Charlie's, I think. It was kind of hard to tell. I was nervous. I felt like an accomplice to a crime.

Aiding and abetting an unexpected driver. Three to five years.

We zipped onto the highway. We zipped into the center lane. We zipped around a couple of cars that were going too slowly.

"I love this tune!" Angelica jacked up the volume on the cassette player and began singing along. "I-I-I'm a foooool for aaaaalllll the wrong reeeeeasons . . ."

Zzzzip. Right lane.

Zzzzip. Center.

Zzzzip. Left.

"Uh, could we go a little slower?" I said.

Now Charlie was singing, too. "But, girl, there's no-o-o foooolin' yoooooou!"

Rrrrrrrrrrrrr . . .

The distant sound of a siren cut through the noise.

Angelica and Charlie fell silent. Angelica's eyes darted toward the rearview mirror.

I spun around. I saw the flashing lights of a police car, gaining on us.

"Oh, great," I said. "Just great!"

"It's okay," Angelica said. "I'll let him go by. It's not for us. It's for another car."

"Who else could it be for?" I said. "No one else has passed us!"

Now the police car was right on our tail.

"PULL OVER TO THE SHOULDER!" shouted a crackly, amplified voice.

"Uh-oh," Claudia murmured.

"You see?" I said.

Angelica was slowing down now. "Switch seats," she hissed to Charlie.

Charlie gave her a Look. "What?"

"When I'm going slow enough, grab the steering wheel and let me slip underneath you," Angelica said. "Then you slide into the driver's seat."

"You've got to be kidding!" I said.

"I can't do *that!*" Charlie protested.

"You have to!" Angelica exclaimed. "I don't have a license."

Charlie's jaw dropped.

The car was on the shoulder now. Slowing down, weaving.

Angelica was in a panic. "Just take the wheel, Charlie!"

Through the windshield, a guardrail loomed closer.

"*Watch out!*" Claudia screamed.

Angelica slammed on the brakes. She yanked the steering wheel to the left.

EEEEEEEEE . . .

The car was fishtailing, heading straight for the rail.

"Aaaaaaaugh!" screamed Claudia.

Or maybe it was me.

I couldn't tell.

With a sickening *CRRRRUNCH*, we hit.

CHAPTER 12

I was flung to the left. My seat belt kept me from smashing against Claudia. It pulled against my waist, squeezing the wind out of me.

The car bounced and struck the guardrail again. It swerved once, twice, then stopped.

"Oh . . . oh . . . oh . . . oh," Claudia kept repeating. Her eyes were wide with shock, her hand open on her chest.

I could see Angelica taking deep, deep breaths. Charlie was holding onto the dashboard, frozen. His face shone with sweat. "Is everyone okay?"

"Fine," Claudia said.

"What do we do now?" I asked.

Angelica unfastened her belt. "Let's switch, Charlie!"

"But — but —" Charlie stammered.

She slid toward him. "Now! Before the police see us!"

Click. Charlie's belt sprang back into its holder.

"Charlie, no!" I said. "*You'll* be the one who gets the ticket —"

Knock-knock-knock.

A burly policeman was rapping on the window.

Angelica swallowed hard.

She rolled down the window.

"Everybody okay?" the policeman asked, gazing into the car.

"We're . . . uh . . . we're fine," Angelica answered. "Thank you very much." She reached for the ignition.

"Not so fast," the policeman said. "Do you know that you were going twenty miles an hour over the speed limit?"

"Twenty?" Angelica squeaked. "Does that mean a ticket?"

"Let me see your license and registration, please."

Charlie reached into the glove compartment. He pulled out a small white computer printout and handed it to the officer. "Here's the registration."

"You're . . . Watson Brewer?" the officer asked.

"No, he's my stepfather. I'm Charlie Thomas. I have my license." He dug that out of his pants pocket and flashed it at the officer.

The officer glanced at it and extended his palm to Angelica. "And you?"

She pretended to search through all her pockets, then said weakly, "I must have left it at home."

"Any other form of ID?"

Angelica pulled out a card and handed it over.

The officer examined it carefully. "You're not seventeen yet. And you're a licensed driver?"

Angelica bowed her head. "Well, uh . . . no."

I had a sick feeling in my stomach. Angelica had tricked us. She'd wrecked the car. She'd put our lives in danger.

"Mr. Thomas, you take the wheel, please," the officer said. "We have some things to discuss at the station house."

"But we're on the way to a concert!" Claudia protested.

I nudged her in the ribs.

Charlie was already scrambling around to the driver's side. He climbed in, sat behind the wheel, and turned the ignition key.

Watson's car sputtered and wheezed. It sounded as if it had the flu. Charlie tried three times, but the car wouldn't start.

"Come with us in the squad car," the officer said wearily. "Lock up and take your keys."

The shock was wearing off. I was beginning to think again.

We were going to a police station. And I had four tickets in my pocket.

An image flashed through my mind. Blade was running onto the stage, before a sellout crowd of screaming fans having the time of their lives. And smack in the middle of it all, right in the choicest part of the house, were four empty seats. While Charlie, Angelica, Claudia, and I sat in a dark, stinky police station in . . .

I looked at the insignia on the side of the police car. STAMFORD.

Hmmm.

That gave me an idea.

Angelica and Charlie were already in the backseat of the police car. Claudia was squeezing in next to them.

"Excuse me, officer," I said. "See, I won this contest — free tickets to the Blade concert? — and it's the only night I can go. And it just happens to be in Stamford. Now, as you saw, my friend Claudia and I did nothing wrong. So, on the way to the station house, would you mind dropping us off?"

The officer chuckled. "We'll see if the chauffeur is available when we arrive."

"Nice try," Claudia mumbled.

We were sunk.

"This is so embarrassing," Claudia said. "Everyone in all the other cars is staring at us. I feel like a criminal."

"We're not criminals!" Charlie retorted.

"*Y-Y-You're* not," Angelica said, bursting into tears.

Charlie put his arm around her shoulders. To tell you the truth, he didn't look so stable himself.

I was expecting a bumpy ride through the streets of Stamford, sirens screaming, lights flashing. But it was a total bore. The officer stopped at every red light and pulled to a safe stop in front of a small, white-brick police building in Stamford.

He marched us into an inner office with dirty white walls, a long table, and a telephone. We sat in chairs around the table.

"Do I — do I — have to go to —" Angelica was speaking in breathless gulps.

"Jail?" the officer said. "No. But what you did was serious. Speeding. Underage driving. Not only were you breaking the law, but you were putting everyone's life in danger on that road. Not to mention causing an accident that someone will have to pay for, and it won't be Mr. Brewer's insurance company. Policies don't cover unlicensed drivers."

Tears were streaming down Angelica's face. "I'm sorry, Officer —"

"Bolton." The officer pulled the phone toward him and lifted the receiver. "Okay, I need to contact all of your parents. Who'll start?"

"All?" Claudia said. "But I wasn't —"

"All."

Once, when we were very little, I was playing with Claudia when she took a stack of twenty-dollar bills from her dad's night table and flushed them down the toilet, one by one. She was waving good-bye to the last bill when Mr. Kishi caught her. It was the only time I ever saw him blow up. To this day I will never forget the look on Claudia's face.

It was exactly like the look she had when the Kishis arrived at the station house.

Officer Bolton carefully explained what had happened. He explained it again to Angelica's parents when they showed up, and again to mine.

I could tell Watson was angry. His entire head was red. Mom looked as if someone had just died.

We were not fingerprinted, or sent to reform school, or interrogated. But Angelica and Charlie both received whopping fines.

The mood was not festive when we left the

station house. Charlie and I didn't even say good-bye to Angelica.

We trudged grimly to the family station wagon. We climbed grimly in. We drove grimly away from the station house. I was tempted to mention the concert, but Watson and Mom both had *no way* written on their faces. So I kept my mouth shut.

No one said a word until we were on the highway again, heading back to Stoneybrook. When Mom finally broke the silence, her voice was soft and choked back. "When the policeman said accident, I thought something awful had happened to you."

"I'm sorry, Mom," Charlie said. "I'll pay for the car."

"The car isn't the important thing," Watson spoke up. "You allowed something illegal and highly dangerous to happen. I would never expect that of you, Charlie."

"But Angelica said she had a license," Charlie said. "I think."

"Watson didn't lend the car to Angelica," Mom reminded him.

"We'll talk when we're home," Watson said. "Some of us need to concentrate when we're driving."

Hoo, boy. When jolly old Watson talks like that, he means business.

It was after eight o'clock when we pulled

into the driveway. Emily was asleep, but Sam, Nannie, and David Michael raced to the front door.

"Are you hurt?"

"What happened?"

"Where are the others?"

The questions flew around us. Poor Charlie had to describe everything, step by step. Nannie was shaking her head in disbelief.

"That was really stupid," David Michael said with this disappointed look on his face.

Charlie nodded. "I know."

"I told Sarah about it," Sam said. "She called while you were away."

"Sarah called me?" Charlie asked.

Sam shook his head. "No, she asked for Kristy. She said she wanted to apologize about something. When I told her you were in an accident, she got upset. She wanted to know if you both were all right. Somebody better call her back."

Watson, Mom, and Nannie were already heading into the house. Sam and David Michael turned to follow them.

Charlie and I looked at each other. "Do you want to call her?" I asked.

"I don't have anything to say to her," Charlie replied.

"Yeah? How about, 'I made a big mistake. I never should have broken up with you'?"

Charlie's face scrunched up into a mask of scorn. "Butt out, Kristy. You leave my personal life alone."

"Fine," I said. "What's Sarah's number? I'll call her."

Charlie turned away and stalked into the kitchen. "Look it up yourself."

CHAPTER 13

"I s he here yet?"

"Nope."

"When's he coming?"

"I don't know. Ask Charlie."

I must have had that conversation seventeen times on Saturday morning at Krusher Klinic. The kids were frantic with excitement.

The "he" they were asking about was Jack Brewster. Old Jack was supposed to show up, but had Charlie given me any details? No.

I'd meant to ask him, but things had been a little explosive at the Brewer/Thomas house the night before. While I was talking to Sarah Green on the phone, explaining what had happened, Watson was giving the Car Safety Lecture of a lifetime to Charlie. After I hung up, I tried to enter the conversation. I, Kristy the Loudmouth, couldn't squeeze a word in edgewise.

If you ask me, Charlie got away with murder. He didn't have to pay for Watson's repairs. He hadn't been grounded. He hadn't been required to compensate me for my tickets — or for my pain and suffering over missing the concert. What was his punishment? Three things. One, he had to pay for his traffic ticket in full. Two, he couldn't drive for a month, not even the Junk Bucket. Three, he had to "rethink his social attachments." (Translated, that meant "find a new girlfriend.") Charlie was not pleased.

I didn't expect him to show up at Krusher Klinic. After breakfast, he'd skulked away, saying he needed to "hang out with buddies" and "clear his head."

Personally, I think he needed to *fill* his head. A few brain cells wouldn't hurt. (I was angry, big time, about missing the Blade concert.)

By the way, Angelica was missing, too. Mr. Hsu had brought his sons to the field.

So, once again, I was running Klinic alone. And I had no idea when Jack Brewster was going to come. Or *if*. For all I knew, "Jack" was a gag. Knowing Charlie, he had planned to spray his own hair gray and put on a Mets uniform himself.

"Listen up, guys!" I announced. "I know you're all excited about Jack Brewster Day, but I'm not totally sure it's going to happen —"

"OHHHHHHHH . . ." The Groan Heard Round the World.

I gritted my teeth. If Charlie didn't bail me out of this one, he was going to be in more trouble than he knew.

"So, until Charlie arrives to straighten everything out," I continued, "pretend I'm Jack Brewster, and show me what you can do!"

I split the players into two teams. As they took the field, I spotted Charlie zooming toward us on his bike.

"There he is!" Jake cried out.

Forget about the game. The kids crowded by the fence as Charlie glided to a stop.

"Where's Angelica?" was his first question.

Can you believe it? I couldn't.

"I have no idea," I replied calmly. "Your players have a more important question for you. About Jack Brewster Day."

"*Jack Brewster?*" Charlie gulped. "Well, um . . . I meant to call my connection. I need to find out if we're still on."

I was cringing. I wanted to throttle him. "In other words, you forgot."

"Look, maybe another day —"

"Tomorrow's the last day of Klinic!" Buddy sounded as if he were about to cry.

Charlie took a deep breath. "I'll . . . I'll make it up to you. Maybe after the season starts."

"Okay, everybody, back into positions," I said gently. "If we pull together today, I propose a team trip to Pizza Express!"

That cheered the kids up. A little.

As they trudged onto the field, my Krushers looked, well, krushed.

Charlie was mounting his bike again.

"Where are you going?" I asked.

"I need to find someone —"

"Angelica?"

"I'll be back!"

With that, he was off.

I kept my temper. I rallied. I ran the most fantastic practice game you can imagine. Charlie or no Charlie.

I didn't even notice when Sarah Green sat in the bleachers to watch. David Michael had to point her out to me.

The night before, I'd explained to Sarah what had happened. She'd said she would try to stop by the Klinic to say hi.

"Snack break, guys!" I announced. "Ten minutes."

As the kids raced to the snack bench, I walked to the bleachers. "Hi, Sarah."

"Hi, Kristy," Sarah called out. "The team looks fantastic."

"Thanks. Charlie helped a lot, you know." Why was I sticking up for him? I don't know.

114

The words just popped out of my mouth. And it was the truth, after all.

"I was hoping I'd see him here," Sarah said.

"Me, too. He's kind of in a weird mood, after what happened."

"I guess he decided against calling my uncle?"

"Who?"

"Well, not really my *uncle*. He's something like a second cousin once removed. You know, Jack Brewster?"

"Your uncle is Jack Brewster?"

Sarah nodded. "That day at the Argo? While you were in the bathroom, Charlie asked me if Uncle Jack would come to the Klinic, so I asked him. Uncle Jack said sure. He's retired, and he loves working with kids. He helps my softball team all the time. Anyway, I left a message for Charlie to call me, but he never did."

"Jack Brewster was supposed to come today!" I blurted out. "Krusher Klinic ends tomorrow."

Sarah thought for a moment. "Uh-oh."

"Do you know his phone number? Could you call him?"

"Sure! It's worth a try." Sarah climbed on her bike, which was propped against the fence, and took off.

I was grinning. I wanted to shout out the news. Kristy's Krushers — my little team —

was going to have a brush with stardom!

Might. *Might.* Sarah was going to call him. That was all.

Still, I was tingly at the thought.

Years of video replays flashed through my mind. Brewster, snagging a line drive, touching third, and firing to first for the triple play. Brewster, breaking up a no-hitter with a clutch two-strike, two-out homer. My dad used to make me watch Jack Brewster in slow motion to help my technique.

I kept it together. I didn't mention a thing during snack time. I managed to herd the Krushers back onto the field.

We hadn't played even one inning before Sarah returned.

She was smiling from ear to ear as she said, "Tomorrow, noon."

"Yyyyyyesss!" I turned to the field and shouted, "Emergency team meeting!"

Have you ever seen the last game of any World Series? The team swarms out of the dugout and mobs the pitcher, hollering and jumping.

Well, that's what happened to me the moment the news left my mouth.

"YEEEAAAAA!"

The Krushers lived up to their name. I was buried alive under a pile of deliriously happy players.

116

Even the parents were impressed. Jamie's dad said he belonged to a fan club called the Brewster Boys. Mr. Pike said he used to comb his hair like Jack Brewster.

When the kids found out that Sarah was related to Brewster, they actually lined up for her autograph. They could not stop chattering.

"Can we get free Mets tickets?" Suzi asked.

"Can we get free hot dogs?" added Jackie Rodowsky.

"Linny Papadakis, plucked from the Krushers to be the youngest player on the Mets' farm team!" Linny said in a corny sports-announcer voice.

Claire's face lit up. "I want to go to the farm, too!"

"Not *that* kind of farm, dodo brain!" Nicky groaned.

Convincing them to play was tough. Sarah helped me. She was great — forceful but kind, helpful but not, well, bossy. She was a good athlete, too. (Which didn't surprise me. It must be in the genes.)

She was the coach I could have used all week.

Once the Krushers got started, they played their hearts out. Even the little ones made plays I'd never have expected of them. The practice flew by.

I have to admit, I didn't have one thought

117

about Charlie — until I saw him. He appeared about halfway through Klinic, standing astride his bike on the sidewalk at the far end of the field. He was just staring, not making one move to come closer.

I was about to yell out to him, when he turned and rode away.

Sarah had seen him, too. "Why didn't he come over?"

I shrugged. "I don't know."

It was a lie. I knew exactly why he hadn't come near us. He was too embarrassed to face Sarah.

The players, fortunately, had not seen him. They kept playing harder and harder. By the end of the Klinic, I was thrilled.

"Krushers, you were sensational," I announced. "I'm going to be proud to show you off to Jack Brewster!"

Linny began a cheer, and the others joined in: *Two-four-six-eight, who do we appreciate — Kristy! Kristy! Yeaa!*

I made them do another cheer, for Sarah. She deserved it.

I was looking at Sarah Green in a whole new way now. I no longer thought she should be going out with my brother.

She was too good for him.

CHAPTER 14

Well, Saturday had been almost perfect. But not quite. As David Michael and I sat on the curb after Klinic, waiting for Watson to pick us up, guess who biked by? (Hint: She was about the last person I wanted to see.)

Angelica came to a stop in front of us. "Hi. I guess I'm too late?"

"Charlie wasn't at Klinic today," I said.

Angelica took an envelope from her pocket. "Would you give this note to him?"

I couldn't believe my ears. She had pulled my brother away from the Krushers all week. Lied about her driver's license. Made me miss the concert of a lifetime. Wrecked my stepfather's car. Almost killed four people. Gotten my brother into trouble with the police. And now she expected me to be her private messenger?

"Deliver your own note!" I snapped.

"It's important, Kristy," Angelica said firmly.

"Very important. Charlie's been leaving messages on my phone machine all day. This is my answer. He needs to read it. If you don't take it, I'll just put it in the mail, and he won't see it for days."

I sat there, not moving. Deciding whether I should talk to her at all. David Michael was looking at me curiously.

"Look, Kristy, I'm sorry," Angelica continued. "I did a really stupid thing, okay? It's not like I haven't suffered. My mom and dad really let me have it. I'm sure they won't allow me to have a driver's license until I'm, like, thirty. If I'm lucky."

"I still haven't heard an apology about the car," I grumbled. "Or the concert."

Angelica sighed. "All right, I'm sorry about them, too. My parents are going to pay for the damage, okay? And I wish I could do something about the concert, but the tickets were free anyway, right? So it's not like you lost any money."

Some apology.

I wanted to knock her off her bike. I wanted to stuff pebbles down her designer shirt. Rip up her note. But I, Kristy Thomas, was above that.

After all, David Michael was there and I needed to set a good example.

Besides, I could tell from her cold, threatening tone of voice that the envelope didn't exactly contain a love note.

And that was just fine with me.

I grabbed it from her hand. "Okay. I'll give it to him."

"Thanks." Angelica pushed off on her pedal and glided down the street.

"She's mean," David Michael said. "But that's okay. So are you."

I burst out laughing. I couldn't help it.

Watson arrived about a minute later, full of his own apologies — about being late. But at least *his* apologies came with a bag of tortilla chips.

As we munched and talked, I eyed Angelica's envelope. Through it I could see computer print. Not handwriting.

Formal.

Something that took extra effort.

What could that mean? A plea for forgiveness? A declaration of love? A homework assignment?

I was *dying* to hold it up to the light and read it.

But I was good. I knew it was none of my business. It was totally between Charlie and Angelica.

When we arrived home, I marched straight to Charlie's room. He was lying on his bed with his door open, listening to music.

I held out the envelope. "This is from Angelica. Want me to read it first, so you know if it's bad or good news?"

Charlie's expression was dull and a little swollen, as if he'd just awakened. "Nah, I'll look at it."

He took it from me and ripped it open. "Probably sending me her speeding ticket."

Lying down on his back, he scanned the letter. I turned to leave. But Charlie began reading aloud.

" 'Dear Charles . . .' " Charlie gave kind of a laughing snort. *"Charles?"*

"That doesn't sound too promising," I remarked.

" 'I haven't called you because I'm really upset,' " Charlie went on reading. " 'I didn't want to cry and yell over the phone, so I figured I'd write instead. First of all, I'm sorry for what I did. It was stupid.' "

" 'Stupid' doesn't come close," I murmured.

" 'My parents are so mad at me. They don't want me to see you ever again. They said it was totally unlike me to do what I did. They think you were a bad influence —' "

"You were a bad influence on *her?"* I blurted out.

"Will you stop interrupting?" Charlie said. He cleared his throat and went on. " 'I argued with them a lot. But then I thought about it. My last boyfriend had a car, too, and I never tried to drive it. Well, he was a great driver, that was the main reason. But even if I asked, *no way* would he have let me. He was this super-mature type. We actually had a lot in common. I think we broke up because we were almost *exactly* alike. Then I met you. You were so dif-ferent — like a big kid. I needed that for awhile. But I have this weakness — I let other people's personalities rub off on me. So what I'm saying is, I think my parents were right. I need to move on, Charlie. I need to find some-one on my wavelength. Hope you're not mad at me. Ciao, Angelica.' "

The words hung in the air, like a bad stink. Charlie fell silent, staring dully at the paper.

"What a conceited creep," I finally said. "She thinks she is so superior."

Charlie let the letter fall to the floor. He grabbed a baseball cap from his night table. Then he lay back and put it over his face. "Leave her alone. Maybe she's right."

"Oh, sure. *You* forced her to drive your car, right? *You* made her crack up Watson's car. As if!"

"I don't mean that part, Kristy. She admitted she was wrong. I mean the other stuff. The im-maturity. Face it, I *am* like a big kid."

"Well, *that's* true," I teased.

"I spend my whole spring break playing

123

softball with my little sister and her littler friends. And I like it. I mean, I *could* be playing baseball with kids my own age. I *could* be doing what normal seventeen-year-olds are doing — looking at colleges, thinking about their futures. At my age, you're supposed to know what you want to do with your life. I don't."

"Isn't that what college is for? To help you decide what you want to do?"

"I look at those stupid brochures, and it's like, 'Huh?' They all look the same."

"You just need to organize them, that's all —"

Charlie peered out from under his cap. "Now you sound like Sarah! She sits around for hours, *ranking* the colleges. She uses about ten different categories. I can't do that. It's like homework. The whole idea puts me to sleep. You have to *want* to go to college, Kristy. You have to be ready. Mature. Not like me."

Whoa. I never thought I'd hear my brother talking about his personal problems to me. Plus, I always thought he *was* so mature. I didn't know he felt like this.

I was tongue-tied. What could I say? My Idea Machine works great for middle-school problems, but it kind of sputters and dies when it comes to stuff like this.

"Well, *I* think you're mature," I said. (I know, big help.)

Charlie laughed scornfully. "Right. You can't even count on me for your Klinic. I'm less reliable than the kids. *They* show up every day. *They* don't just walk away from practice whenever they want."

"Well, wait until they have boyfriends and girlfriends —"

"Remember what you told me the other day when I left Klinic? You told me I was just like Dad."

I cringed. I wanted to kick myself for saying that.

"Charlie, I was angry. I didn't mean it."

"Well, guess what? You were right. I've been thinking about this a lot. It's all in the genes, I know it. If Dad were a musician, I'd probably be in a rock band. If Dad were a writer, I'd be working on the school newspaper. But what is Dad? Immature and messed up. I'm going to be a big grown-up baby the rest of my life. That's it. Done deal. Can't change it."

"Stop it! You're nothing like Dad!"

"Yeah, right —"

"Charlie, do you remember what happened after Dad left?"

"Duh. No, I forgot the worst day of my entire life. Of course I remember."

"To me, it was like the end of the world. Meltdown. The sky is falling. I'd never cried so hard."

"You'd never cried until then," Charlie said with a little chuckle.

"Mom was a basket case."

Charlie nodded. "She was hit the worst. David Michael had colic. Sam was totally out of it. How many times did he ask 'When's Dad coming home?' Seven zillion? I can't believe Mom didn't slug him."

"You managed okay."

"On the outside, sure. Someone had to. I couldn't just let the family fly apart."

"You were only ten then. And you were making all the decisions."

Charlie laughed. "One time the bank called about the mortgage payment, and I made Mom teach me how to write a check."

"I remember you waking up in the middle of the night to feed David Michael."

"I had to. Mom was exhausted."

"Mom says she doesn't know how we would have survived without you."

"I didn't even think about stuff like that. I was just trying to make up for Dad being away."

"Pretty mature for a ten-year-old."

"I guess."

"Do you really think you've changed that much?"

"Why should I —"

Charlie cut himself off. It was as if a stopper had been shoved into his mouth.

We sat there for a long while, without saying a word.

"Look, Charlie," I said. "I don't know what to say about colleges. I wish I did. But I can tell you one thing. Whenever I'm stuck with a big problem, if I'm losing my temper or feeling pressured or just at wit's end, one question pops into my mind."

Charlie smiled. "Where's the ice cream?"

"No," I replied. "Every single time, I ask myself, 'What would Charlie do about this?' And usually I come up with the right answer."

I turned to leave. I thought I saw Charlie's eyes moistening. I wasn't sure, though. Because mine were.

CHAPTER 15

"That's it, Nina. Now, just lift up your back elbow a teeny bit."

Nina Marshall shyly obeyed the suggestion. Her knees were bent slightly, her back was tilted forward, her legs planted wide apart. For the first time, she looked like a real honest-to-goodness player.

She'd never followed *my* instructions like that.

But then again, I'm not Jack Brewster.

Yes, the great day had arrived. The Krushers' brush with fame.

Practice had never been so crowded. For one thing, every single father had shown up (*that* was a Krusher first). Some brought friends. I didn't recognize half the adults there. I had to ask them to back away from Jack Brewster so the kids could ask him for autographs.

Word must have leaked out among SMS students, because a whole gang of them had gathered, too. Alan Gray had brought a stack of index cards for autographs. Brewster had signed about three before I caught Alan and chased him away. (I heard him yelling, "Get yer autographs, five dollars each!" The dork.)

Oh. Guess who had called me the night before, all buddy-buddy? Bart Taylor. It was a "Hi-is-it-true-about-Jack-Brewster?" kind of call.

I guess he'd canceled his clinic for the day. Because he and his whole team showed up to watch ours. Hmmm . . .

The Krushers, needless to say, were ecstatic. The Barretts and Kuhns had fresh haircuts for the event. Linny and Matt wore brand-new baseball cleats. Seven Krushers had scrawled Brewster's uniform number, 41, on their T-shirts. (Jamie wrote 14, but he's learning.)

As for Jack Brewster, he was nothing like what I expected him to be.

I had this mental image of him from the old videos. Young, lean, and fierce-looking. A black mustache, rock-solid jaw, and dark sunglasses.

Well, the mustache was gone. So was most of the hair, and what was left was grayish. The fierce expression had melted into a craggy, kind smile. He looked like . . . an uncle.

And he paid as much attention to the smallest Krusher as he did to the biggest.

Nina swung the bat and almost fell over. But she hit the ball up the first-base line.

"Fantastic!" Jack Brewster exclaimed. "Give that girl a contract!"

Nina was beaming. "My mommy wears contracts, but she changes to glasses at night."

"Me, too," Jack Brewster said with a laugh. "Well, we've all batted around now, so let's have a fielding practice! Charlie, you hit. Kristy pitches and Sarah catches."

All this time, Charlie had stayed to the left of Jack Brewster. Mainly because he was nervous about being near Sarah, who was on Brewster's right.

No, Charlie still hadn't talked to her.

Sigh. Maybe he wasn't as mature as I'd thought. (Well, at least he wasn't moping about Angelica anymore. And he'd been looking at college brochures again over breakfast.)

Jack Brewster assigned positions to the Krushers. Charlie took some practice swings in the on-deck circle, not looking at Sarah, who was catching my warm-up pitches.

"Okay, batter up!" shouted Jack Brewster.

I lobbed a pitch to Charlie. He took a huge swing, but the ball bounced weakly to second base.

Laurel picked it up and threw to first.

"Great throw!" Jack Brewster shouted. (Laurel looked as if she'd just met Santa Claus.)

"Charlie," Jack Brewster said softly, "your wrists are quick, but you need to work on follow-through. Kind of the opposite of Sarah's problem. Sarah, would you stand behind Charlie and take him through the last part of the swing?"

Sarah stood up from her crouch. Looking cautious and uncertain, she stood behind Charlie. Then she reached around, taking his forearms.

Slowly she helped him through his swing, leveling out the last part of it. I thought for sure Charlie would be embarrassed.

But I could see the corners of his lips turn upward into a smile. Just like Sarah's.

Come to think of it, Jack Brewster was smiling, too.

I may be wrong, but I think he knew something.

I think Sarah had talked to him.

Which was just fine with me.

And, clearly, with Charlie, too.

Dear Reader,

Mind Your Own Business, Kristy! takes place during spring vacation. Kristy's family isn't going away, so Kristy plans Krusher Klinic for her softball team. When I was growing up, my family often visited our relatives over spring vacation. Sometimes we visited Louisville, Kentucky, to visit my father's family. And sometimes we went to Florida to visit my mother's parents. The trips were always lots of fun. My Florida grandparents lived across the street from a big lake. My sister and I could go fishing from their dock. Best of all, we kept our eyes peeled for alligators. They really did live in the lake!

Mom's parents lived in Winter Park, which is very near Disney World. My sister and I had visited Disneyland when I was thirteen, and we loved it. Unfortunately for me, Disney World wasn't completed until I was in college. So I didn't get to visit it until I was an adult, and I was researching *Baby-sitters on Board!*, the first BSC Super Special. What a fun reason to visit Disney World for the first time.

Happy reading,

Ann M Martin

Ann M. Martin

About the Author

ANN MATTHEWS MARTIN was born on August 12, 1955. She grew up in Princeton, NJ, with her parents and her younger sister, Jane.

Although Ann used to be a teacher and then an editor of children's books, she's now a full-time writer. She gets the ideas for her books from many different places. Some are based on personal experiences. Others are based on childhood memories and feelings. Many are written about contemporary problems or events.

All of Ann's characters, even the members of the Baby-sitters Club, are made up. (So is Stoneybrook.) But many of her characters are based on real people. Sometimes Ann names her characters after people she knows, other times she chooses names she likes.

In addition to the Baby-sitters Club books, Ann Martin has written many other books for children. Her favorite is *Ten Kids, No Pets* because she loves big families and she loves animals. Her favorite Baby-sitters Club book is *Kristy's Big Day*. (By the way, Kristy is her favorite baby-sitter!)

Ann M. Martin now lives in New York with her cats, Gussie and Woody. Her hobbies are reading, sewing, and needlework — especially making clothes for children.

Notebook Pages

This Baby-sitters Club book belongs to _____.

I am _____ years old and in the _____

grade.

The name of my school is _____.

I got this BSC book from _____.

I started reading it on _____

and finished reading it on _____.

The place where I read most of this book is _____.

My favorite part was when _____.

If I could change anything in the story, it might be the part when

_____.

My favorite character in the Baby-sitters Club is _____.

The BSC member I am most like is _____

because _____.

If I could write a Baby-sitters Club book it would be about ____

_____.

#107 Mind Your Own Business, Kristy!

When her brother Charlie falls in love with a not-so-great girl, Kristy has to decide whether or not to mind her own business. Kristy thinks Angelica is bad news. This is what I think of Angelica: _____

_____. The perfect girl for Charlie

would be my friend _____, because

_____. I had

to mind *my* own business once when _____

_____. I *didn't* mind my own

business when _____

_____. This is what happened to me: _____

_____.

Kristy makes a fuss because she cares a lot about Charlie. A person

I care a lot about is _____. If I thought

he or she was in love with the wrong person, I would _____

_____.

KRISTY'S

Playing softball with some of my favorite sitting charges.

A gab-fest

Me, age 3. Already on the go.

SCRAPBOOK

...with Mary Anne!

My family keeps growing!

David Michael, me, and
Louie — the best dog ever.

Read all the books
about **Kristy**
in the Baby-sitters Club series
by Ann M. Martin

THE BABY-SITTERS CLUB

Look for #108

DON'T GIVE UP, MALLORY

I'm usually a good speaker, with a loud, clear voice. But not today. Today I could barely read, let alone talk.

" 'I do not like them in a house,' " I continued reading. " 'I do not like them here or there.' "

Mr. Cobb, who had been standing behind me, cleared his throat and interrupted, "Valerie, you skipped 'I do not like them with a mouse.' "

I stared down at the page, totally confused. How could that happen?

I reread the page, this time very slowly, to make sure I didn't miss any words. Behind me I could hear Benny Ott making snoring sounds, as if I were putting him to sleep.

My ears, my cheeks, my freckles — my entire

body was flaming beet red. I could hear a rushing sound in my ears.

While my mouth was reading the words, my brain was screaming, "Please, take the book from me — give it to someone else!"

Rrrrring!

I froze in midsentence. Was that really the bell or had I just imagined it?

All around me kids were standing up. Mr. Cobb was walking to the front of the room.

The bell had really rung. Hooray!

I bolted from my seat and charged for the door. I should have returned the Seuss book to Mr. Cobb. But I left it on my desk. I knew if I spent one more second in that classroom, I'd scream.

Once out of the room, I raced to the girls' bathroom and splashed water on my face. How could so many things go wrong in one class?

First, Mr. Cobb hadn't even noticed me. Then when he did, he had my name wrong, which was really humiliating. Then kids teased me about my good grades. But when I was asked to read out loud to the class, something I've always been really good at — I choked.

I raised my head and looked in the mirror above the bathroom sink. "*Valerie* Pike," I murmured to my reflection. "It fits. Valerie, the-totally-mixed-up, Pike."

THE BABY-SITTERS CLUB®

Collect 'em all!

100 (and more) Reasons to Stay Friends Forever!

More titles... ▶

The Baby-sitters Club titles continued...

☐ MG48226-2	#82	Jessi and the Troublemaker	$3.99
☐ MG48235-1	#83	Stacey vs. the BSC	$3.50
☐ MG48228-9	#84	Dawn and the School Spirit War	$3.50
☐ MG48236-X	#85	Claudi Kishi, Live from WSTO	$3.50
☐ MG48227-0	#86	Mary Anne and Camp BSC	$3.50
☐ MG48237-8	#87	Stacey and the Bad Girls	$3.50
☐ MG22872-2	#88	Farewell, Dawn	$3.50
☐ MG22873-0	#89	Kristy and the Dirty Diapers	$3.50
☐ MG22874-9	#90	Welcome to the BSC, Abby	$3.99
☐ MG22875-1	#91	Claudia and the First Thanksgiving	$3.50
☐ MG22876-5	#92	Mallory's Christmas Wish	$3.50
☐ MG22877-3	#93	Mary Anne and the Memory Garden	$3.99
☐ MG22878-1	#94	Stacey McGill, Super Sitter	$3.99
☐ MG22879-X	#95	Kristy + Bart = ?	$3.99
☐ MG22880-3	#96	Abby's Lucky Thirteen	$3.99
☐ MG22881-1	#97	Claudia and the World's Cutest Baby	$3.99
☐ MG22882-X	#98	Dawn and Too Many Sitters	$3.99
☐ MG69205-4	#99	Stacey's Broken Heart	$3.99
☐ MG69206-2	#100	Kristy's Worst Idea	$3.99
☐ MG69207-0	#101	Claudia Kishi, Middle School Dropout	$3.99
☐ MG69208-9	#102	Mary Anne and the Little Princess	$3.99
☐ MG69209-7	#103	Happy Holidays, Jessi	$3.99
☐ MG45575-3		Logan's Story Special Edition Readers' Request	$3.25
☐ MG47118-X		Logan Bruno, Boy Baby-sitter	
		Special Edition Readers' Request	$3.50
☐ MG47756-0		Shannon's Story Special Edition	$3.50
☐ MG47686-6		The Baby-sitters Club Guide to Baby-sitting	$3.25
☐ MG47314-X		The Baby-sitters Club Trivia and Puzzle Fun Book	$2.50
☐ MG48400-1		BSC Portrait Collection: Claudia's Book	$3.50
☐ MG22864-1		BSC Portrait Collection: Dawn's Book	$3.50
☐ MG69181-3		BSC Portrait Collection: Kristy's Book	$3.99
☐ MG22865-X		BSC Portrait Collection: Mary Anne's Book	$3.99
☐ MG48399-4		BSC Portrait Collection: Stacey's Book	$3.50
☐ MG92713-2		The Complete Guide to The Baby-sitters Club	$4.95
☐ MG47151-1		The Baby-sitters Club Chain Letter	$14.95
☐ MG48295-5		The Baby-sitters Club Secret Santa	$14.95
☐ MG45074-3		The Baby-sitters Club Notebook	$2.50
☐ MG44783-1		The Baby-sitters Club Postcard Book	$4.95

Available wherever you buy books...or use this order form.
Scholastic Inc., P.O. Box 7502, 2931 E. McCarty Street, Jefferson City, MO 65102

Please send me the books I have checked above. I am enclosing $_____
(please add $2.00 to cover shipping and handling). Send check or money order—
no cash or C.O.D.s please.

Name_____ Birthdate_____

Address _____

City_____ State/Zip _____

Please allow four to six weeks for delivery. Offer good in the U.S. only. Sorry, mail orders are not available to residents of Canada. Prices subject to change.

BSC5962

THE BABY-SITTERS CLUB®

by Ann M. Martin

Collect and read these exciting BSC Super Specials, Mysteries, and Super Mysteries along with your favorite Baby-sitters Club books!

BSC Super Specials

BSC Mysteries

More titles ➡

The Baby-sitters Club books continued...

Available wherever you buy books...or use this order form.

Scholastic Inc., P.O. Box 7502, 2931 East McCarty Street, Jefferson City, MO 65102-7502

Please send me the books I have checked above. I am enclosing $ _____
(please add $2.00 to cover shipping and handling). Send check or money order
— no cash or C.O.D.s please.

Name_____Birthdate_____

Address _____

City_____State/Zip_____

Please allow four to six weeks for delivery. Offer good in the U.S. only. Sorry, mail orders are not available to residents of Canada. Prices subject to change.

BSCM496

The New THE BABY-SITTERS CLUB® FAN CLUB

Only $8.95!
Plus $2.00 Postage and Handling

Sign up now for a year of great friendships and terrific memories!

- ★ **110-mm camera!**
  Take photos of your pals!
- ★ **Mini-photo album**
  Fill it with your best pics!
- ★ **Diary (with lock!)**
  For your favorite memories...and secret thoughts!
- ★ **Stationery note cards and stickers**
  Send letters to your far-away friends!
- ★ **Eight cool pencils**
  With the signatures of different baby-sitters!
- ★ **Full-color BSC poster**
- ★ **Subscription to the official BSC newsletter***
- ★ **Special keepsake shipper**

Amazing stuff!

PHOTOS